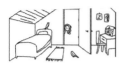

THE ORPHANS' HOME

Inspiring Stories From
Janusz Korczak's Orphanage

MICHAL BEN GAL

Producer & International Distributor
eBookPro Publishing
www.ebook-pro.com

THE ORPHANS' HOME
Michal Ben Gal
Copyright © 2023 Michal Ben Gal

Translation: Noelle Canin

Illustrated by Ron Levin

Contact: mbengal@studio-2.co.il

ISBN 9798388907424

All the stories you will read here are as close to the truth as possible and did indeed take place at or around the orphanage.

Itzchak Belfer was 98 when this book was written. Janusz Korczak raised him from the age of seven and he accompanied my writing with sound advice, adhering as much as possible to what really took place there, at the orphanage in Warsaw.

CONTENTS

HOW IT ALL BEGAN

When the decision was made to build a Jewish orphanage at 92 Kruchmalna Street in Warsaw, Poland, Dr. Janusz Korczak participated in its planning.

One rainy day, the doctor arrived for a meeting at the architects' office in Warsaw. A checked scarf was wound around his neck and his spectacles were foggy with cold. He was thoroughly excited to be part of the planning of the orphanage he himself would run.

Uncharacteristically tense, he stood in front of the distinguished Polish architects, some of whom were the greatest in the world in their field. A serious man, he had a small reddish beard and kind eyes.

"I envision a building with plenty of spacious areas and large windows that let in an abundance of light, hope, and warmth," he described his vision in detail to the experts. "Large openings generally indicate an open mind and therefore, gentlemen, yes, yes, large openings are a good thing." Behind his round spectacles, his eyes sparkled in response, but his expression remained serious. His name as a doctor, writer, and war hero preceded him in Poland and he was respected by a great many people.

He continued: "So, as I said, I want a home with wide windows and stairs, everything must be wide, parquet flooring and..."

One of the architects, a small man with an impressive mustache who was puffed up with pride, rose to his feet and interrupted him, saying loudly: "Excuse me, sir! I have planned a building with wide interiors painted in pure white. The white interiors will make the house appear larger."

Korczak listened patiently until the architect had finished speaking and then replied: "Forgive me sir, but I don't like white interiors. I don't want the house to look like a hospital. Believe me, I have spent a great deal of time in hospitals and know from experience that it would only bring me and the children depression and despair."

The men around the table shifted uneasily in their chairs. Some of them nodded in agreement but the architect with the mustache, who appeared to be the leader of the group, bristled and his mustache seemed to stretch like a fine rope about to tear.

Korczak, who was essentially a conciliatory man, hurriedly added in a soothing tone: "This building will be the most beautiful orphanage in Poland. I wouldn't want it to be like the soulless buildings constructed today. The sketches are so beautiful. I'm sure the laughter of children will spring from the large interiors you have designed. Regarding the color white, the walls will get dirty very quickly as the children won't keep them clean and what a pity to waste all that beauty. Let's find a compromise, sir, for the sake of the wonderful home you are designing," ended Korczak, smiling at him.

It was impossible to resist the famous doctor's shining eyes. The man with the mustache was mollified and they continued to plan the house in detail, including the large surrounding garden. From his experience as a pediatrician, Korczak knew that nature was beneficial for people, and he was always looking for ways and opportunities to connect children with nature's magic and mystery. He found that the encounter with nature bore real results, whether in a forest or on the banks of a river, on a bench, or merely looking out at the green landscape beyond the hospital window. He even relied on pictures of landscapes, trees, and flowers, which he always had nearby to calm a distressed patient.

"Nature will calm the anger and sadness of orphaned children who come to the house. I have to include the wholeness of nature in this orphanage!" He said movingly, concluding with a captivating smile.

"What else do you envision for the house, sir?" Asked one of the architects.

Rising, Korczak began enthusiastically to describe the house he envisaged: "I'd like a grand piano somewhere central, there perhaps?" He pointed at the sketch of the huge hall at the entrance of the house. "I envisage the children sitting and playing, I can actually hear the sweet sound of their music filling the house." He thought for a moment and added in a more practical tone: "Naturally, it's important the piano stand in a protected area so the weather won't destroy it."

Korczak suddenly got up and stood on a chair, saying in a loud, clear voice: "I want each and every child to have an opportunity for change. With your help, honored architects, we can do this," he looked at the people sitting around the table and said: "You are gifted, you will plan us a house where the children can be happy and self-confident, able to make a mistake and admit it, thus growing up in the most beneficial way."

There was something magical in someone who found the good in each child, someone who related seriously to each child. Korczak maintained a dialog with the children through writing, story-telling, singing, and listening. At that moment, he was standing on a chair and explaining quietly and persuasively how they could create a dialog with children by means of designing a home for them.

QUALITY TIME
WITH THE DOCTOR

"Doctor, you're wanted!" A loud cry surprised them all. It was a gray wintry day in February and heavy clouds lay over the orphanage. A group of children were skating on the ice in the courtyard. It was late afternoon and despite the bitter cold, Korczak and the children were engrossed in play and skating antics. The janitor watched over the smaller children who were skating and constantly falling.

A sudden cry was heard: "May I speak to Doctor Korczak, please?" When Korczak heard his name called, he hurried over to the gate, his scarf billowing behind him. In front of the gate he saw an elderly woman standing with a boy or girl – Korczak's spectacles were so fogged up with cold, he couldn't see clearly. The two were dressed in thin shabby clothes that were certainly not suitable for such a cold day.

The woman stood bowed, a woolen hat on her head.

The boy (or girl's) hair was uncovered, dirty, and fell to the shoulders. The boy's face was black and dusty, his white teeth stood out against his dark face and a tear was engraved in his cheek. "I've heard about the orphanage," murmured the woman. "You have to help us," she said, gently pushing what turned out to be a boy in Korczak's direction. He, the boy, apparently understood why he'd arrived at the door to the orphanage.

He didn't say a word. Expressionlessly, he went in through the gate and met Korczak's eyes. The children exchanged knowing looks: another child had come to live with them at the orphanage.

This wasn't how children were accepted by the orphanage. The family usually met with Korczak in his attic room for an introduction and a conversation. But there were also other instances, some children even came alone to the orphanage. They arrived neglected and hungry, and it was impossible not to take them in. The orphanage was known throughout Poland as a home worth growing up in, far more than other disreputable orphanages.

Korczak exchanged several sentences with the woman who then quietly backed away and went off again into the bitter cold. He took the child into the orphanage. It was pleasantly warm in the room and the sweet smell of Sabbath bread baking filled the house. Korczak quickly wrapped the boy in a blanket and asked his name. "My name is Marcelo," murmured the boy in a quiet voice.

"Marcelo, glad to meet you," the doctor extended his hand. He didn't care that his hand was stained by the child's small dirty hand.

"Have something to eat, Marcelo," the doctor poured out hot tea and handed him one of Stefa's famous sandwiches, all the while talking to him as pleasantly as if he'd known him for years. He knew how to draw children out from the moment he met them. The children, who had had a similar experience, knew that Marcelo would be entranced by Korczak and would swiftly tell him everything he'd gone through.

That evening, Marcelo would be the first to shower. It was Friday, several hours before Kabbalat Shabbat (the receiving of the Jewish Sabbath). It was the day the doctor cut the boys' nails and, if necessary, their hair. Every Friday, Korczak insisted on doing this himself. This was how he could look at each and every child individually, this time with the diagnostic eyes of a doctor. Every child was examined by his shrewd eyes, unaware that he was being examined by a doctor.

Marcelo went into the hot shower with explicit instructions on how to use the soap, how to wash his hair and dry it properly: "Press your right thumb into your neck and rub...a lot of dirt is concentrated there." Quickly, while instructing him, Korczak helped the child to wash his hair with circular motions. The water that splashed down off the child's body was black.

"Marcelo, I'm going to give you a smart haircut!" Declared the doctor in a funny voice. While cutting his long, matted hair, the doctor began talking and joking with the child. "Marcelo, I'm drawing the map of Warsaw on your head. Here, this is the orphanage, the market, and here's the school," he chatted, his fingers holding the scissors and swiftly cutting his hair.

While cutting, the doctor examined Marcelo's hair. Was it thick? Coarse? By the nature of the hair, Korczak judged the boy's character and what he'd been through until then. Had he been taken care of? Did he have a family? In the meantime, the boy was motionless, enjoying the attention and pleasant stroking of his hair.

Later, in his small handwriting, the doctor would write down all his impressions in a notebook, those of a shrewd pediatrician who examined and diagnosed the neglected child. In a few days' time, he'd examine him again, comparing the information on the chart to see if he'd improved.

"Now we'll cut your nails." As usual, like any child in the world, Marcelo wasn't happy about this, but he already trusted Korczak and held out his fingers with their long nails.

The other children listened to what was going on behind the door. Each one remembered how he himself had been in that position when he'd come to the orphanage. "I won't hurt you, don't worry," said Korczak, gently cutting the boy's nails, rounding the edges so they wouldn't cut into the skin, explaining to him why it was important not to bite one's nails.

In the meantime, the boys waited to go into the shower and enjoy a private conversation with Korczak. This ceremony was important for him and for them, but they respected the reception of the new boy and the long private time he spent with the doctor.

Marcelo was given a pair of shoes and if he thought

the ceremony was over he was mistaken. The doctor reappeared, this time with a brush and shoe polish. "Look, Marcelo, this is how you'll hold the shoe and the brush. See, this is the amount of polish to smooth onto the shoe."

The boy nodded, standing in front of the doctor. Thin and sensitive, his hair cut short, he now looked exactly like a boy.

He approached the mirror and gazed at his image as if seeing himself for the first time.

When he laughed, his white teeth no longer stood out against his face, which was in fact pale.

Marcelo left the bathroom and was immediately swallowed up among all the children, becoming one of them. In the meantime, it was Kobusz's turn to enter the bathroom. Kobusz was happy, he now had the doctor to himself, quality time. He'd collected several important things during the week to tell him.

THE LIGHTHOUSE KEEPER'S ROOM

Dr. Korczak had his own room up in the attic. The children respected his privacy, but they knew that if one of them didn't feel well, had a temperature, or was simply in a bad mood, he could go to Korczak's room and lie down to rest on the sofa there. Korczak occasionally invited one of the children, but they frequently came to him of their own accord.

Tamar was a street child, her hair was light and wild, her slanted eyes were green, and she was all legs and mischief.

Korczak assigned an older mentor for each new child to teach them house rules and customs and to accompany and support them for several months. Tamar also had a mentor but even after six months she still found it hard to adjust to the strict house rules. Tamar only shared her difficulties with her mentor, Yirczka. The role of a mentor involved great responsibility and only reliable children were chosen for the task.

Yirczka explained to Tamar that nobody went up to the attic without permission from Korczak. Because of this, Tamar, who always had to test things for herself, particularly if they were forbidden, felt she had to go up there. For several days now, her eyes had followed Korczak every time he'd quickly mounted the stairs to the attic. What was up there? She asked herself. Maybe up in the attic, there was a magical room full of shining things? Or maybe there were wild animals, like the ones in the stories the Doctor told them? Or perhaps he had another family there with polite, well-combed children who spoke an educated language and didn't curse or argue like the other children in the house? She had to go up, just once, and peep in. Peep in and go downstairs again at once. Yirczka had explained to Tamar that if she asked Korczak if she could go up to his room or if she just knocked on the door, he'd be glad to see her, but she was shy.

One morning Tamar was ill. Although she could have gone to school with the others, a devilish and mischievous voice whispered inside her: "Tamar, you have a golden opportunity, there aren't any children in the house and all the adults are busy...this is the very time to go up to the attic to see what is in there."

When the last slam of the door was heard after the last child had gone, quiet prevailed in the house. All the adults were occupied and Tamar began to make her way upstairs. She quickly passed along the long, closet-lined corridor, stood at Korczak's door, and peeped inside.

To her great astonishment, she saw an ordinary room with a low, sloping ceiling. The room reminded her of a lighthouse keeper's room. Inside was an ordinary bed, beside which stood a simple dresser, a table, and a tall chair. On the table was a model of the orphanage on which were glued the children's milk teeth that had fallen out. Korczak had a regular habit: whenever one of the children lost a tooth, he'd buy it from them. Tamar even saw her own large milk tooth that had fallen out two weeks before when Korczak had enthusiastically bought it from her. She felt rather proud when she saw her tooth at the top of the strange sculpture standing on his table.

In the room was a window that had a large railing and overlooked the orphanage. On the windowsill stood dunnocks, common street birds. Tamar was immediately drawn to the large window, the light that streamed in, and the good air blowing into the room.

She heard a sudden rustling. And there in the corner of the room stood a cage of mice. And who was sitting stroking the mice? Who if not the doctor?

Tamar gasped in alarm.

"Why! I have a guest!" Holding barley in his hand, the doctor gazed at her. He approached the window and put the barley on small plates scattered along the windowsill. "Come Tamar," he called to her, "come and see how they survive. Street birds are brave and strong, just like human beings."

"Did you know that I observe them and learn about them?" continued the doctor. "Sometimes sparrows come too, they can't dig for food with their beaks, so I put out food for them on little plates. Come and put out some food for them."

Tamar approached and picked up some of the barley in her small hand.

"You know, I knock on the door before I come into the room. The birds hear me and aren't alarmed. Once, I didn't knock and one of the sparrows was injured. It's always a good idea to knock on the door before entering."

"That's true," agreed Tamar. She was embarrassed.

The doctor continued to speak; he noticed her embarrassment but felt no need to dwell on it. It was clear to both of them that she wouldn't enter his room again without knocking.

"I know that sparrow, it's fat from all the food it eats and chases away the other birds. Do you see those two sparrows over there? They're quiet and polite and dislike fighting, they sit peacefully waiting for me to feed them."

Tamar cautiously approached, stretching out her hand to feed the two sparrows. Afterward, she spent hours in the attic, watching Korczak fill his notebooks with comments about the birds. She was so entranced by the street birds that she almost forgot to look around and see what was in the room.

"Look, doctor, that's my sparrow! See how cheeky it is. Not afraid of anything, it's actually sitting on me!" Tamar laughed, happier than she'd felt in a long time.

Only when she heard the lunch gong did she go downstairs, hand in hand with the doctor.

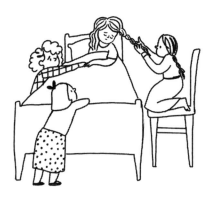

THE MENTOR

As was the case with Tamar, in order to ease the absorption of new children, Korczak assigned each child a mentor for a period of three months. The mentors were older children who had shown themselves to be responsible and had gained the trust of the Children's Council. The Council consisted of nine children who were annually elected and, among other tasks, it was responsible for assigning mentors. The mentors' role was to show and explain house rules to new children, helping them adjust to the institution's framework and to the group. The mentor was usually, but not necessarily, older than the new child. The concept behind mentoring was that new children might find it easier to confide in and consult a slightly older child than an adult. Mentors saw their role as highly significant, one that carried a great deal of responsibility. It was an opportunity to experience caring for others, an experience that was both enriching as well as enlightening.

Helenka, who volunteered to become a mentor was selected by the Children's Council and began to mentor Renia.

The mentoring was very successful but, three months later, Helenka went to Korczak and, to his surprise, asked to continue mentoring Renia for another three months.

"Three months is usually long enough for a child to get used to the house with a mentor," thought Korczak. "Why change routine?"

When he talked to Helenka, Korczak realized that the request was important to her personally and not to Renia. After some deliberation, he reluctantly agreed.

Helenka again approached the task of mentoring with responsibility and maturity. She had a small notebook in which she noted down various events that occurred in the course of Renia's week, describing her nature and qualities. When she consulted Korczak to make sure she was behaving correctly with the child, she'd refer to the notebook and her comments. She'd sometimes note down Korczak's comments. In short, there was no more serious mentor than Helenka.

When three more months had passed, Helenka's role came to an end and again she approached Korczak and asked to mentor another child. This time, Korczak hesitated. He believed the mentoring was a burden for her. He'd observed her during the six months she'd mentored Renia, feeling that she took her job so seriously that she didn't allow herself to be a child. Helenka laughed, fooled around, and played a lot less, all because of the heavy responsibility involved in her mentoring role. Finally, Korczak couldn't resist her pleading and again submitted her name to the Children's Council. They were all unanimous in choosing her again because she really was very special, responsible, and serious.

0Mira relied on Helenka for everything and thus three months of mentoring passed quickly. Mira adjusted, began to wander about the house on her own, and understood the system of rights and obligations in the house. She gradually found her place. She began to play the piano and sing aloud in a bell-like voice. The boys, enchanted by her beauty, began to take an interest in music and would sit listening to her play.

The months of mentoring came to an end. Helenka again requested to volunteer as a mentor. The children held a secret vote this time too and, to her amazement, her request was denied.

"You've been a mentor several times, now it's the turn of other children to take on this role," she was informed by the Children's Council. She went to Korczak and tried to convince him, but to her surprise he, too, stood firm in his refusal. "Helenka, there are other roles in the house, other tasks you can do. The decision is final."

Thus, for the first time in long months, Helenka had nobody to look after. She couldn't get up in the morning as she didn't feel needed and had no reason to get up. Helenka was depressed. The younger girls tried to help her. They would stroke her hair, sing to her and tell stories, but she lay in bed shut away in her own world. Even when she did get up, she barely spoke. Mira was worried. From time to time, she'd look at her, not knowing how to help.

That week, Mira was on wake-up duty, a very responsible role, which required her to get up earlier than everyone else and wake them on time.

Every morning, the doctor would go up to the bedrooms very early, while everyone was still asleep. One morning, he saw Mira standing at the bedroom window, breathing in fresh, cold air, tears in her eyes. He approached and stroked her hair.

"Off you go, Mira'leh, wake up the girls. You'll be late for school." Mira began to carry out her wake-up duties. The girls got up, all except Helenka, who huddled under her blanket. It was a cold day, but the girls were disciplined, made their beds, washed, dressed, and went downstairs.

Mira approached Helenka's bed, stroked her, and murmured gentle, soothing words.

"It was me who asked the children not to let you mentor again," Mira whispered to Helenka, her lips trembling, "maybe I was wrong."

Helenka was astounded. "Didn't you have a good time with me?" She asked, even more heavy-hearted than usual.

Mira looked at Helenka with eyes that expressed such deep feeling that Helenka felt that anything she said now, no matter what it was, would greatly surprise her. She waited for her friend to speak.

"I also asked Korczak not to let you mentor again," said Mira, continuing before Helenka had time to respond. When my parents died, I was left alone with three young brothers. They were younger than me, but I was also young! Too young to take care of three little ones. I did the best I could," whispered Mira hoarsely. "I was like a mother to them, but I myself was just a girl." Mira raised her eyes to look directly at Helenka. "I took care of them like you took care of me. Until we were taken, I came here and my brothers were adopted by a family, I had forgotten that I myself was a child. I won't let you make the same mistake I made. You're older than me but not much older. You're also a child, like me. I've learned to play again here, to chatter, even be bored."

Mira fell silent. Helenka was also silent. "Don't you realize that we love you like a friend? I love you and want you to be the older sister I never had. We can help each other and pretend we're real sisters. What do you think?"

Mira knelt down, her beautiful face raised to Helenka, her eyes full of tears and unconditional hope. Helenka, who was "just" a child, wept. She'd never wept before, was always as strong as a rock, and suddenly things were overturned. Mira'leh sat on the edge of Helenka's bed and looked after her like a mentor. Like a loving mother.

When they came down to the dining room, Korczak smiled at the sight of little Mira'leh enveloping the tall Helenka with love, Helenka's face looking like that of a baby who had just wept bitterly.

"Sometimes it's good to let children take matters into their own hands without interference," he thought. He sat down for breakfast at one of the tables and was swallowed up among the chattering children.

THE VOTE

Szymon was a tall, black-haired child with huge feet that contrasted with his skinny body. He'd arrived at the orphanage two months previously. Every time a new child arrived at the orphanage, Korczak would have him lie down on a sheet of paper spread out on the floor and sketch the outline of his body. He'd measure his height, his weight, and foot size, after which he'd prepare various graphs and tables according to his findings. He did the same for Szymonek (his nickname in the orphanage).

Korczak observed him more than any other child while writing down data in his notebook. This child undoubtedly preoccupied the doctor and researcher of child illness. He couldn't pinpoint the illness from which Szymonek suffered, but his sense that something wasn't right with the boy floated stubbornly in the air.

Szymonek's behavior was strange, robotic, and almost mechanical. He talked a lot, but there was something strange and robotic about his speech as well as if it were a machine speaking, and not him. A machine with a great deal of unlimited knowledge, one that always knew what to say, but not when or how. One that says everything in a monotone – questions and answers, explanations and jokes – everything sounded the same.

The children felt that his behavior was strange and tried to get closer to him because they knew he wanted friendship but didn't know how to ask for it. Korczak noticed Szymonek's behavior and was moved to see the children's desire for his company. He initiated plenty of opportunities for Szymonek to connect with other children, particularly in situations where he could demonstrate his great, general knowledge.

Reuben was Szymonek's mentor. He was a Jewish student who was employed as a young counselor in exchange for food and board. He had a notebook on which Szymonek's name was written in large letters and there he noted events related to his protégé. He was responsible for following up and reporting on his behavior to Korczak. Three months after his arrival at the orphanage, Reuven would have to make a recommendation concerning Szymonek, according to which the children would decide whether or not the new protégé would remain at the orphanage and what his status would be. Likewise, the boy had a permanent mentor who was a little older, whose name was Izrael, and who was responsible for his adjustment to the home and, mainly, the learning of his rights and obligations.

Despite great help from Reuben and Izrael, Korczak was

very worried. He saw no significant change in Szymonek's behavior. The child was different! Korczak was concerned that the children wouldn't choose him as one of the group. He shared his concerns with his partner Stefa: "What will happen if they don't choose Szymonek to live with us? How would a child like that receive rejection? What would happen to him outside the orphanage? Maybe there's another framework that would be more suitable for him than our home? Should we influence the children's decision?" Korczak wondered.

Stefa nodded, great pain in her eyes. She remembered an incident the month before when a child called Pikolek had hurt other children. He was transferred to another framework. Every child who was made to leave the home broke Stefa's heart. In the case of Szymonek, it hurt her twice as much, because she knew the child wasn't normal and that everything he did was done in all innocence and he wasn't aware of his singularity.

Korczak shared his concerns about the lonely child with Izrael and Reuben. "In two days' time, the children will vote on whether or not to let Szymonek stay in the home, I'm concerned that they won't vote for him. What do we do? How can we help him? I'm really worried about the results of the vote."

Reuben the counselor responded: "Doctor, I'm trying to help Szymonek. I teach him how to behave but he doesn't always listen to me. He offends the children and doesn't notice when they're hurt. I just don't know what to do."

The mentor, Izrael, nodded gravely, saying: "And I repeat rules of behavior with him. Yesterday, I sat with him and we did role-play. He simply doesn't see others. Maybe you can help me, Doctor, because I'm at a loss."

Korczak nodded sadly. "To me, it sounds as if you're doing all the right things with him. Szymonek needs a lot of role-play, a lot of explanations. He lacks things an ordinary child takes for granted. I'm also very worried about him because no one outside our home will be able to devote the attention to him that he needs. However, just like any other vote, I'm not going to interfere and will allow the children to decide."

Izrael and Reuben looked defeated. They sighed, and Izrael said: "We all know what will happen. Can we really not guide the children in their vote? Just this once?"

Korczak stood up, thus ending the conversation. "Friends, enough! Don't be upset. What needs to happen will happen, but we have rules in our home and we must abide by them. These rules constitute the foundation of the home. The children's right to determine by democratic vote who remains here carries a heavy responsibility, I won't give up this fundamental principle."

The little meeting ended and each one left deep in thought, regret, and concern.

Two days later the day of "publication" arrived – the day on which all those with the right to vote would determine, or not, the acceptance of a new child into the orphanage. This time the vote concerned Szymonek staying. The vote usually created tension for the new student. Every new student understood the importance of improving and maintaining good behavior because his friends had the right to determine if he stayed with them or not.

The moment arrived. There was tension in the air. Each child received a note on which they had to mark a plus if they recommended Szymonek staying in the home, and a minus if they thought he should leave. The number zero indicated they had no opinion on the issue. At the end of the vote, Korczak counted the votes and put the results up on the notice board. His face was expressionless.

An hour later, the students rushed to the notice board to read the results of the vote. Szymonek sat in the quiet room, drawing in silence, he didn't appear to care about the vote that concerned him. The children gathered around the board in great amazement. On the board was one uniform response from all the children. This had never happened in previous publications – they all, without exception, had voted unanimously.

Korczak stood there contemplatively. He appeared to have learned a great deal from the children's decisive statement. Korczak learned something about his students, Szymonek, and about himself. He approached Szymonek and whispered the results in his ear. Szymonek smiled, skipped on his big feet straight into the large hall, repeating: "I'm staying with you. I'm staying..."

THE PRINCESS &
THE "PRINCE AND
THE PAUPER"

Korczak believed that education didn't only take place in school. He tried to take the children out on a variety of extra-curricular cultural activities. Stefa and the doctor applied to the heads of the Jewish Community in Warsaw and, every week, they received a contribution of 20 tickets to the cinema. They also received tickets to the circus, theater, and various exhibitions.

That day, the children in the orphanage received tickets to the cinema in honor of mid-year school certificates. Korczak loved the cinema, he both enjoyed watching movies and using the medium as another way of observing the children's minds. He would explore their response to the movie and was always attentive to the way in which he

could use the movie to benefit some process.

Nitza, a yellow-haired girl with a scattering of freckles on her face, burst through the door and ran to the girls' dormitory. Her face red, she flew upstairs.

Six months previously, Nitza had come to the orphanage from a broken home. Her mother had died when she was born, and her father was an alcoholic. She had wandered the streets on her own, occasionally begging for food. When the Jewish community heard about this, they removed her from her neglected home and brought her to the orphanage. Even now, after six months in the orphanage, she was still very far from being a regular student. She hadn't even known how to read or write when she'd arrived. Korczak spent hours with her in the quiet room, trying to teach her school rules. He assigned her a personal mentor as he did with all the children, but asked the mentor to take responsibility for the area of learning as well. The mentor taught her, but she didn't improve much.

Nitza started to get ready to go to the movie. She put her certificate with its low grades, to say the least, on her bed. She put on her good blue dress with the white dots, swiftly braided her hair, and was about to go downstairs when Korczak and Stefa suddenly entered the room and sat down beside her. Stefa complimented her appearance. "What beautiful braids," she said, and Korczak added: "What a charming dress, Nitzush'keh. You look like a princess." They talked for a few minutes before going down to the large hall together. As they got up to go, Korczak said casually in his quiet voice: "Nitzush'keh, don't return your schoolbooks to the storeroom today, you will need them next year."

Nitza listened and was silent for a few seconds until Korczak's words sank in. A weight fell from her heart. She was relieved. Since she'd received her certificate, she'd been worried. What would Korczak say? How would Stefa feel? It hurt her to disappoint these two beloved people who had adopted and nurtured her for the past six months. She glanced at them both and saw only love in their eyes. Nitza took a deep breath of relief, calmed down, and bravely accepted the decision to spend another year in the fifth grade. Taking a deep breath, she ran down to the group of children waiting for her.

The children were wearing their best clothes and complained to her: "You're always late." They opened the door and went out into the yard, running out through the gate. Nitza was swallowed up in the joyful group.

They all hurried after Korczak. They were always infected by his great enthusiasm and this time he was as excited as a child. The movie the children were about to see was a favorite of his – "The Prince and the Pauper." He'd seen the movie at least six times. He jogged along at the head of the group and, in all the hurry, kept having to readjust his glasses that kept slipping off of his nose.

Before taking the children to see a movie, Korczak made sure to see it himself, either alone or with a friend. Afterward, when accompanying the children back from the movie, he had time to observe them and see their responses. They were mostly fascinated by what was happening on the screen. Korczak asked the children for their responses: "Had they enjoyed it? What did they enjoy? What made them laugh? What made them cry? Korczak was curious to see how Nitza had responded to the movie. She had a unique and developed imagination and her naïve and childish responses impressed him.

When they reached the cinema, Korczak addressed Julius the usher as usual. He asked him how he was progressing with his studies and he knew all about his personal issues. The children entered the hall and Korczak whispered to Nitza: "Come and sit next to me Nitzush'keh. And if you find it hard and want to leave, I'll go with you." And so, they started to watch the movie "The Prince and the Pauper."

Nitza knew the movie they'd see that day was a particularly sad one. She'd overheard Korczak consulting Stefa about whether or not to take the little ones to the movie. She'd even heard them discussing how the sad movie would impact her, Nitza, a sensitive child.

Now she sat absorbed in the screen among all her friends. They watched the stories of two 16th-century, English children. Tom Canty the pauper, whose father was a drunkard and whose wicked grandmother abused him, and Edward, the spoiled son of a king. The two children looked alike and, after a random, chance meeting, decided to exchange places, clothing, and roles. Tom remained in the palace and Edward went out into the tough London neighborhoods. Tom, whose father was always beating him, insisted on learning to read and write and knew how to manage in his new world as a prince.

At the beginning of the movie, Nitza covered her eyes and blocked her ears. It was particularly painful for her to watch the parts when Tom was beaten by his father, but, gradually, she opened her eyes. She closely followed Tom the pauper's story as he managed to learn and become a different person.

In front of his eyes, Korczak saw Nitza change. Even the color of her eyes grew stronger and deeper. He could actually sense it: She raised her head and watched the movie with uncharacteristic courage. Her hands no longer covered her ears but were clasped tightly together. Her cheeks shone with joy and renewed health. When the movie ended, Nitza gave Korczak her small hand. Together they walked back to the orphanage.

Bedtime was approaching and, on the pillow, Nitza would soon encounter the certificate that had so disappointed her a few hours previously. "Don't worry," Nitza suddenly said to Korczak, she herself surprised by her daring. "I will succeed at school next year." Korczak squeezed her hand. Nitza smiled, adding: "Want to bet on me?"

Korczak allowed "bets" at the orphanage. Every Saturday after breakfast, the children would come to him and bet that their behavior would change within a period of time they determined together. They'd quarrel less, lie less, or argue less. He relied on bets to mobilize the children to avoid wrongdoing and take responsibility for their actions.

He was very happy that Nitza initiated a bet with him. "Of course!" Said Korczak and squeezed her hand. "Come on, let's make a bet. We'll bet that you get over a 70 average."

"No, at least 80," replied Nitza.

"75?"

"80", she insisted.

Korczak smiled and wrote down the bet in his notebook.

CURSES

Henryk arrived at the orphanage after living on the street for a year. He was a real lawbreaker and had no family to take care of him. Good people in the Jewish community brought him to Doctor Korczak at the orphanage. He was a small boy, though muscular and solid. His brown hair was sun-streaked, his black eyes burned with rebellion, and his mouth was a fountain of curses.

He cursed a lot, but Korczak noticed his excellent capacity for articulation, if you could listen in between the curses. Every time he saw the child, Korczak thought to himself how good-looking he'd be if he only smiled a little. He hoped he would see him smile in the home.

He decided to play a game with the children, particularly with the boys. "Want to make a bet?" From time to time, he'd approach and challenge them. Once a week they'd come to Korczak and make a bet with him on all kinds of things. Every bet was written down in a notebook and, a week later, if they won the bet, they'd receive a candy or two. He asked Selek, Julius, Israel and Natek, Haim and Josef, he asked everyone: "What do you want to bet on?" So, very gradually, all the children got used to the custom.

Selek made a bet with Korczak: "I will only hit someone once a day this week!"

"Excellent!" said Korczak. "If you succeed, I'll give you two candies."

Julius made a bet with him: "I'll only forget things five times this week."

"Excellent!" replied Korczak, and wrote down the bets in his notebook.

Israel made a bet: "Tomorrow at school, I'll tell my teacher that she wears ugly clothes."

"Very interesting," said Korczak, as he hummed to himself and noted down the bet.

Chaim made a bet with him: "I'll go and visit my parents tomorrow and won't pay for my tram ride." This bet was also recorded together with all the others.

The purpose of the bets was to help the children identify habits they wanted to get rid of and slowly stop them. A child who won the bet would be challenged by Korczak again, thus further reducing unwanted behavior. Korczak didn't like some of the bets, but at that point he wrote them all down without changing anything.

Meanwhile, Henryk would watch from the side, utter a juicy curse and go back to his affairs. "All that effort for a candy?" he'd scoff to himself. But Korczak saw that every time Henryk took one more step towards the group, his cursing grew less.

A few weeks had passed since the betting game started and, one morning, for the first time, Henryk approached the betting booth. He walked slowly, unconfidently, saying with great seriousness to Korczak: "I bet you that this week I will only curse seven times."

"Seven times! Maybe six?" Said Korczak indifferently. "It's a bet!" He added, noting down the bet. He didn't show the children how happy he was, especially not Henryk, when a child finally approached him and participated in an activity with the other children. Each week, Korczak's notebook filled up with a great many bets.

On Friday morning, the cook sent Korczak to the market for last-minute purchases before the Sabbath.

"Come with me, Henryk," Korczak invited the boy. Henryk quietly approached him, blurting out some small curse, but his face expressed such sweet, naïve wonder that Korczak had chosen him for the walk. As usual, Henryk's face was sour and he walked beside Korczak, looking around with suspicion. Several months had passed since he'd wandered the streets, and memories of hard days living on the street, hungry and without a roof over his head, overwhelmed him with a wave of anger. But then, without intending to, he held out a hand to Korczak and they walked together in silence until they reached the market.

The smells were intoxicating. Fruit, perfumes and spices. Everything was so shiny and well organized as if a painter had gone by and painted every fruit and vegetable with a brush. Peddlers' voices rose into the air: "Tastier with me!" "Cheaper with me!" "Healthier with me!" Everyone seemed to know the doctor, and they all tried to tempt him to buy something from their stall.

The doctor nodded a greeting to one and all, speaking to each one, asking how they were: "How is your son, Leon?" He asked the pot-bellied greengrocer. "And what about your father? Has he recovered?" He asked Dunya, owner of the herb stand. Korczak shook hands with everyone, thumping them on the shoulder as if he knew each and every one at the market. All the peddlers were glad to talk to the pleasant, dignified man who took such an interest in them.

Henryk was entranced. He felt as if he were in another world, one full of charm, taste, smells. and sounds. He held Korczak's hand tightly. He'd never seen the market so full of people. He always slipped in at night to look for food in the empty market. Actually, it was with all the commotion around him that he felt calm and peaceful.

How come everyone knew the doctor? Henryk thought to himself, feeling proud that everyone admired his doctor.

"Hey, doctor, we have a competition today!" Called out the whiskered butcher in his hoarse voice. He wore a white, stained apron, and had a smile on his face.

"What competition?" Korczak pretended surprise.

Henryk sensed that Korczak was teasing the whiskered butcher and that he knew exactly what competition he was referring to.

"Our cursing competition," said the butcher. "Remember?"

"Of course, I remember!" Said Korczak. Fetching two stools, he placed Henryk on one of them.

"It's against the rules to repeat a curse," reminded the butcher and started the competition.

For an entire hour, the two uttered curses which Henryk, who had grown up on the street, had never heard before. In different languages, with strange sounds, and varying colors and rhythms.

Henryk suddenly felt that with each curse he heard, another curse dropped from his mind forever. As if he were disconnecting and, in the end, he'd be left only with the diamond Korczak hoped to discover in him.

Finally, they grew tired. The butcher slowed down and the curses that came out of their mouths became increasingly strange. People in the market gathered around the two competitors and encouraged them. Some encouraged the butcher whose enormous black mustache trembled with exhaustion. Others encouraged Korczak, who laughed like a child and fired curses in all directions, occasionally examining little Henryk's reactions as he sat elatedly beside him, tears of laughter coming out of his eyes. He had never laughed so freely.

The pace of the curses continued to slow down. It was Korczak's turn to curse, but he seemed to have run out of curses. Then, in a loud voice, the butcher uttered his most unique and final curse: "I will swallow you down until nothing is left. Not even a crumb!" Korczak laughed. He knew how to lose, and joyfully too.

When they returned to the orphanage, Henryk looked at Korczak through different eyes, as if seeing a naughty side to his nature, which not all the children knew. He realized that he also enjoyed betting with himself. Korczak also observed the boy, sensing that someone different, cleansed, was walking alongside him. As if he'd emerged purified from the fun in the market, which was crowded, dirty, and noisy. "Strange," Korczak thought to himself. "In that of all places, the diamond emerged from the boy."

Some days later, it was time to note down the children's new bets. Every child approached Korczak with their bets. Henryk was last. He approached Korczak and told him: "Let's bet that I will never curse again, I've heard enough curses this past week."

Korczak gazed at him, at his sun-streaked brown hair, his black eyes burning with love and trust, at his smiling mouth. He was actually smiling. "If you win this bet," said Korczak, "I'll...I'll swallow my hat until nothing is left. Not even a crumb!" The children didn't understand the meaning of Korczak's sentence, but Henryk did and laughed freely for the second time in his life. Of course, he'd win.

M...MY NAME IS A...
ANNA!

Anna didn't speak at all and the children living with her in the orphanage didn't understand why.

Anna was a thin small child with fair, almost transparent skin, a sprinkling of ginger freckles on her pale face. Her eyes were usually downcast but anyone who succeeded in meeting her gaze saw a pair of dark eyes that were black and bleak. Her father fell ill and since there was no one to provide for the family, Anna and her siblings were sent to various orphanages. Every night Anna dreamed the day had come when her entire family would be reunited.

The State Jewish school was at no. 61 Gjibovska Street. There they learned Polish and most of the teachers were Jewish. Some of the students were Jewish children who had grown up in the area, while others were students from Janusz Korczak's orphanage. The Korczak children always looked different from the others: Their appearance was tidy, and they were good students, very polite and self-confident.

One day, at the beginning of the year, the teacher asked Anna her name. The first time she received no answer, the second time she asked slightly irritably, and the third time Anna answered in a whisper: "M...m...my n...name is An...na."

Many of the children burst out laughing, but Korczak's children were silent. Each of them had led a troubled life, and now they felt compassion for the humiliated girl who was one of them. They suddenly realized why she didn't speak. Hannah, her mentor, reddened and looked down in shame. How come she hadn't seen it? How come she'd missed it and thought the child was shy?

Doctor Korczak and Miss Stefa had noticed Anna's stammer when she first came to the home. They'd seen how withdrawn the girl was, how she shrank whenever someone approached her. Hannah, her mentor, was helpless, not knowing how to open her heart. With the insight of a child, she'd hug her, hold her hand occasionally and talk to her all the time. Naturally, the conversation was one-sided. Hannah would talk and Anna would nod her head.

That afternoon, on their way home, the streets were cold. There were dark clouds in the sky and a cheerless wind whistled outside.

After their meal, the children played inside. The yard was empty because they were all curled up in the warm rooms, each child busy with their own affairs. Korczak, who had heard about what had happened in class, felt the time had come to talk to Anna. He'd intended to give her a few more days to adjust, but now he decided he could no longer delay the conversation about the "elephant in the room." Like a large elephant trying to hide, Anna's stammer was now known to everyone, and nobody dared to discuss it.

Korczak regarded Anna with his kind eyes and called her to a talk in the yard. "Annushka, come into the yard. It's quiet there and we can talk."

Anna followed him without a word.

Korczak and Anna sat beside each other on a bench in the garden. Korchczak's nose was red with cold and his spectacles were covered in fog. He tightened his red scarf around Anna as well, and they sat there, close to one another. "Annushka," he said, "I see that you stammer. Does it bother you?"

Anna nodded. A small tear rolled down her cheek.

"Listen, my little girl, almost a tenth of children stammer. Boys stammer more than girls, at a ratio of four boys to one girl, and three-quarters of the children who stammer will stop of their own accord. Only one percent of children, a hundredth, will continue to stammer as adults. Anna, you will not be among the one percent, I promise you!"

Silence.

"You want to stop stammering, right?"

Anna nodded. She glanced at Korczak.

Korczak continued: "Tomorrow, you will take a letter from me to your teacher in which I will write that you must not be called to the board, all your exams will be written not verbal, and if there is no choice, you will be examined verbally by the teacher in another room."

"From this moment on, we will help you here at home – Stefa, myself, Hannah your mentor, and all the children. We will all help you."

Anna was silent.

Korchak added: "From today, I suggest you try and read aloud on your own so that you can hear your own voice. Find a vacant room, there are many rooms in the house and simply practice. Sit and read aloud repeatedly. If by chance someone enters the room – stop reading."

From that day on, Anna could be seen going into the quiet room or the small shop at the orphanage, into the kitchen if the cook wasn't there, or the dormitory when the girls weren't there, and reading to herself aloud from books she loved.

The children, pretending they couldn't hear, heard clearly that when she read a text to herself, she didn't stammer at all.

Anna didn't realize that the children could hear her. A week later she didn't care that Hannah heard her, two weeks later Ludvika and Judith played nearby, and a few days later, she didn't even notice who was in the room. She simply stood and read to herself aloud. She felt that the entire orphanage, from the children to the staff, stood behind her and believed in her. She persisted in the task she'd been given and gradually improved.

In the middle of the school year, a young, new teacher arrived at the school. On her first day, she stood nervously in front of the class. Hesitantly, she began to ask the children their names.

"My name is Anna," responded Anna in a steady,

confident voice. "Welcome to our school!" She added, raising the first smile on the young teacher's face.

On their way home that spring day, the children surrounded Anna with a special request: "Anna, won't you go on reading to us aloud? We want to hear more of the wonderful stories you read to yourself and to us."

WITH YOUR PERMISSION, I'D LIKE...

With your permission, I'd just like to explain...

From the testimony of Itzchak Belfer, who was raised by Janusz Korczak: "We had a special list for fights. It was on the notice board and so anyone who wanted to fight a friend would write down his own name, the person he wanted to fight, and when. In the event that a fight broke out spontaneously, without prior intention, we'd put ourselves on the list afterward. The notice board was extremely important to us because that's where the list of our house chores was put up, our daily schedule, and important notices. There were requests we had as well as requests for forgiveness."

This story, inspired by Itzchak Belfer's testimony, took place on a wintry Sunday.

In the last month, several new boys arrived at the orphanage from various places in Poland. Among them were children who were weak, quiet, and very shy, and there were also several rebels. Children who were angry with everything and everyone, with the whole world, and had difficulty accepting house rules.

Everything was frozen outside. The children were full of energy but had nowhere to go. There were occasional days in winter when they could go out into the backyard, have snowball fights or skate on the ice, but that week it was too cold.

Tall muscular Jašek and burly Meitek were new boys at the orphanage. Both were constantly angry. Jašek had a black tuft of hair and a white face, and Meitek was a short, but strong red-head. Like two roosters, the two constantly sought reasons to quarrel, trying to draw more and more friends into their group. Guided by Korczak, the counselors stayed close to keep an eye on what was happening. From time to time, when they felt the atmosphere heating up and that a fight might break out between the two, one of the counselors would say to them: "With your permission, I would like to..." and he'd suggest something that would postpone the fight to a later date.

To better understand the story, it's important to remember that meals in the orphanage always took place quietly, in an orderly and pleasant way. One team was responsible for serving food, another would clear the tables, and even the direction the servers took when serving food was taken into account. Food was served from right to left, in order to prevent collisions and accidents among the servers. A student on duty would conduct the movement of the servers and it was his role to make sure everything was done properly.

The dining room was on the entrance level, whereas the kitchen was in the basement and was connected by a small dumbwaiter. Kitchen attendants would load it with food that would be manually pulled up to the dining room with straps, where servers would remove it from the dumbwaiter and hand it out to the children. At the end of the meal, they'd clear the tables and put the dishes in the elevator. It was hard physical work, and only strong children were chosen for this duty.

That Sunday, at lunchtime, everyone was astonished to see that Jašek and Meitek were dining room attendants. Mosek, the senior counselor, was going past when he saw them quarreling and arguing again, this time about their work.

"I'll pull everything up by myself, I have the strength. I don't need any help." red-headed Meitek shouted angrily.

"You won't manage it alone, your arms are too short," Jašek laughed.

Meitek's arms really were short in relation to his broad body. And everyone nearby laughed, which angered him even more and he reddened with rage.

Wanting to calm them down, counselor Mosek said: "With your permission, I'd like to suggest you hold the elevator on both sides and pull up the food together." The two did stop fighting and did as he said, but were clearly unhappy with the situation.

When the children had finished eating, Jašek and Meitek

began to load the elevator with dirty dishes to lower it to the kitchen, and again began to fight and argue. This time the little elevator rocked slightly but the boys didn't notice. They were so engrossed in their quarrel. Korczak saw what was happening and approached them as if by chance, saying to them: "With your permission, I'd like to suggest that Meitek load the elevator with dishes in an orderly manner and Jašek will help lower it. Just make sure it is balanced because otherwise, the elevator might drop down." He made his suggestion and went away.

Mosek, who was responsible for making sure everything was done properly, passed the two bickering boys several times, and again repeated: "With your permission, I'd like to suggest..." but despite the many good suggestions, Meitek and Jašek did not get on.

Suddenly a tremendous noise of dropping and crashing was heard – the little elevator dropped and disintegrated. The two on duty who were busy with their new quarrel, didn't notice that the rope had slipped out of their hands and the elevator had slid down with all the dirty dishes in it.

The noise of the crashing dishes and the warning bell of the elevator were dreadful. Red-headed Meitek, who until that moment was completely red, now turned white and white-face Jašek turned completely red. Korczak went up to them and said quietly: "With your permission, I'd like to suggest that you put your names on the notice board on the fight list. Then he left.

The two children angrily went off to the list of fights on the notice board and registered their names for a fight on Thursday at four o'clock. The notice board was full, so they knew they had to wait five days for their fight. They parted and each angry boy went off in a different direction.

In the coming days, Jašek and Meitek continued to report to the kitchen for duty at the elevator. They knew there was a date for their intended fight, so they guarded their anger and worked diligently together. The elevator, which had been fixed, descended and ascended without any unnecessary shock. Mosek occasionally went past the two but they didn't appear to need his suggestion. Korczak, too, went by, muttered something unintelligible to himself, and left.

Redheaded Meitek and Jašek became a wonderfully effective team. Since they were both strong, the work was done twice as quickly in half the time. Everyone followed them with their eyes on Monday, Tuesday, and on Wednesday nobody could believe it. Meitek and Jašek began to appear half an hour before kitchen duty, just to talk. And when they finished, they'd lean on the clean and tidy elevator, tired but satisfied after their work.

Meitek suddenly said to Jašek: "Tomorrow's Thursday, remember? We're signed up for a fight at four o'clock." I remember, replied Jašek. Now they knew each other. They'd discovered they had things in common and enjoyed playing the same games. They didn't want the fight. Sitting on the steps at the entrance, they thought about what to do in the fight set for the following day. Korczak, who went past by chance, looked at them and said: "With your permission, I'd like to suggest ..." "Cancel the fight!" They shouted in unison. They jumped on each other, joyfully rolled about on the floor like two puppies, and didn't stop laughing.

PIANO DUTY

For the children's benefit, it was preferable to set simple, clear rights and obligations and so there was a daily schedule in the home. The day began at a fixed time in the morning and ended at a fixed time at night when the students went to bed. In the course of the day, there was time for play, reading and enjoyment, and time for carrying out duties. Each student in the home had defined obligations.

The orphanage was maintained by the children, under the watchful eye of Miss Stefa of course. Thanks to the children's chores, only a housekeeper, one janitor, one washerwoman, one seamstress, and one cook were needed. There were plenty of educators because Korczak's students helped with education.

Every three months, Korczak would hand out postcards to the children on which to note down things to be remembered like something achieved through effort and perseverance, meeting a goal, or some special event.

On one side of the postcard were pictures of special landmarks in Warsaw, or the River Wisła, and others. On the other side, in his beautiful script, Korczak wrote the reason for receiving the postcard: Rising on time on winter mornings, helping friends, carrying out duties, and more. The children learned that all work was respected. Korczak signed each postcard himself. The children worked hard for his postcards and whoever received one kept it safe in their personal drawer.

Shar'keh was a frail and sickly little girl who wasn't physically strong but she, like the others, shared the assumption that everyone could contribute, and that none of the children should live at the expense of others. She didn't want to be different. Korczak knew she couldn't do duties like cleaning the steps, polishing the floor, or handing out heavy food trays. He was, after all, a doctor and noticed her frailty.

One day, he decided to give her a chore her frail body could deal with: dusting the black grand piano in the hall. Shar'keh was overjoyed and gave everything she had to the job. From time to time, after the piano shone under her devoted hands, Shar'keh sat down to play something. At first, she was hesitant, her fingers brushing the keys, but in time, she remembered the tunes she knew, and she sometimes spent an hour playing the piano. "Her piano", as she said to herself.

Shar'keh was sometimes jealous of other children who had more than one chore, and who kept several postcards they'd received over the years in their personal drawer. Sometimes they accumulated about thirty cards in three years.

One day, they sat together on Helenka's bed, looking at her accumulation of postcards. Helenka excelled at everything she did. Her postcards revealed her character. She loved nature and, for her work in the vegetable garden, she received thirteen postcards with pictures of beautiful landscapes. She loved cooking and for her help peeling potatoes, she received seven postcards. She loved to help, and for polishing shoes, she'd received four postcards. She also excelled in her studies and received a postcard for her success at school. Suddenly, while browsing through Helenka's postcards, when Shar'keh was trying to overcome her jealousy, Helenka jumped on the mattress, all the postcards, and Shar'keh, jumping with her.

"You know, Shar'keh," she said, panting from her jumping. "I'm jumpy, but I've noticed that when you play your piano, it makes me feel calm. It's since you've been playing in the background while I do my homework. And I've also noticed that your playing in the morning helps everyone to get up, not just me." She landed back on the bed and sat down beside Shar'keh, kissed her cheek, and ran downstairs.

Shar'keh thought about the things Helenka had said and hoped they were true: "Do I really help the children? Despite my weak and sickly body, is there really something that calms others?"

This conversation with Helenka infused Shar'keh with power. Every morning she was among the first of the girls to get up. She didn't wait to be called, not even in that cold winter, she immediately got dressed and ran to the piano, which had become her "good friend." She talked to it and told it all her secrets while she wiped a damp cloth over the 88 keys. The children who were still in bed heard the piano strings and woke to sounds of a magical melody.

Many days passed, until one morning, Shar'keh ran as usual to the piano but found it shining as if someone had only just wiped it clean. On the piano, she saw a postcard. Her heart beat with excitement. She approached and saw that the postcard was for her and written in Korczak's curling handwriting:

Dear Shar'keh,
I, your friend the grand piano, am giving you a postcard for taking good care of me. For 250 days you have come every morning, in all weather, and kept me clean. Because of you, I give pleasure to everyone in the home and succeed in making the children feel calm, even the naughtiest of them. Thank you very much.
The Piano.

Shar'keh was overcome with joy. The feeling that she was useful was wonderful. The postcard she held in her hands seemed the prettiest of all the postcards she'd ever seen. She felt like playing and wondered if the keys under the lid had also been cleaned that morning. She lifted the lid of the piano to clean it, and to her astonishment saw about a hundred postcards, on which was written: The Children's Council has decided to award this postcard for helping a friend," or for "making a friend feel calm," or "for help with the wake-up call," or "helping with homework." A different reason was written on each card and each one was signed by a child in the home. The pictures on the postcards were different from the others, and were in all the colors of the rainbow, with the best reasons for their being given to Shar'keh. She sat down to play and her small hands lovingly caressed the 106 postcards.

She collected all the postcards together with an elastic band and put them in her personal drawer. That evening she and Helenka will sit on her bed and look at all her postcards, she thought happily to herself.

THE SYMPHONY

"Abrasha, come and play outside!" "Abrasha, come on. What's keeping you?!" Every time Abrasha played his violin, these voices accompanied his playing.

There was a small room in the orphanage that served as a store for office equipment, and this was where Korczak and Stefa allowed Abrasha to practice his violin every day. He had remarkable talent and Korczak believed that it was important to reinforce every child's inherent gift.

Abrasha was a grave-faced boy with black hair and sad, brown eyes. He glanced outside into the backyard and watched the children ice skating. He looked down at the violin beneath his chin that was already addressing him: "Abrasha, you're staying in to play me, you're not going outside." And, indeed, Abrasha very quickly forgot the commotion outside and without hesitation continued to play.

The violin frequently saved him from loneliness and

longing and he felt he had to be as loyal to it as to a good friend. Something else attached him to the violin: He knew the doctor loved music and listened to him playing from wherever he happened to be at the time. That day Abrasha was practicing a technique called "Spiccato." He bounced his bow back and forth and was absorbed in his task until he heard the dinner gong.

"Abrasha, come and sit next to me!" His friends' voices intruded on the sounds of the exercises he'd been playing all day. He was a popular boy and everyone loved him, although they weren't pleased with his preference for playing the violin rather than playing with them.

Korczak sat eating with a group of children. At a certain point, he rose to his feet and everyone fell silent. "Friends," he said. "Today there will be auditions for the main role in a new play. We are putting on a musical for Hanukkah (Jewish Festival of Lights) next month. Ester'keh and the counselors will watch the auditions with me.

Ester'keh was responsible for theater and everything related to it: She built the set and sewed the costumes and she also managed the actors' rehearsals.

Everyone knew that Korczak attributed great importance to the process of producing a play in the orphanage because the varied work enabled different children to show their strong points: Acting, playing an instrument, singing or sewing.

Korczak would invite important donors to the performances who would come to learn about the orphanage and who were in a position to help maintain it.

Abrasha listened to Korczak and was infused with a

competitive spirit. He instinctively knew he'd be chosen to play the lead. Closing his eyes, he disconnected from everyone and tried to remember – what had the previous plays been about? He tried to imagine the subject of this year's play and whether he could play his beloved violin.

After dinner, Abrasha returned to the little room and held his violin again. He closed his eyes and began to play. He imagined himself shining on stage in the lead role. Gradually, other visions appeared in his mind. He remembered the day he'd arrived at the orphanage. He was hungry and afraid, and how he'd encountered Korczak's benevolent eyes. He also remembered how in time, Korczak had realized his musical talent and noticed his long, beautiful fingers. "The fingers of a violinist," or so Korczak had once said to him, and Abrasha was filled with pride. "I know what to give you when you lose your first milk tooth," promised Korczak. And, indeed, when Abrasha's first tooth fell out, he received a wonderful gift – the violin that belonged to the home. Although the violin wasn't his alone, everyone knew and heard that it was primarily Abrasha who took care of the violin.

When it was time for the auditions, Abrasha left the little room. Everyone was already in the hall. All the children were tense. All the boys hoped to get the lead role, that of a boy this time. A new boy, whom Abrasha barely knew, stood out. The boy sat on the edge of his seat, ready and nervous about the audition. There was something special about that boy's face, something Abrasha liked. "The face of an actor," he defined it to himself.

All the counselors came to the audition for the lead

role and, naturally, Stefa and Korczak. The subject of the musical was "The Story of the Maccabees" and, since it was a musical, the first to audition were children who could play instruments.

Abrasha's turn came and he went up on stage with his "good friend" in his arms. He closed his eyes and began to play. Through the music rising from the violin, there arose dreams in his heart for a better world where there was no poverty or suffering, where everyone had enough to eat, something to wear, and a warm home with a soft bed and white sheets. He dreamed his father and mother were smiling at him, hugging him, he dreamed of playing games with his younger siblings, about a huge world filled with people he'd play for and who'd rise to their feet, enthusiastically cheering him.

He dedicated every sound he made to the doctor and to Stefa. He forgot he was auditioning, only grateful for the possibility given him to live with dignity and to be special. While he was playing with his eyes closed, he suddenly heard the sweet sounds of a harmonica. It was Shmulik Gogol. And there was Jenna on the piano, then Dudek on the mandolin and Leon on the accordion. An extraordinary symphony of gratitude was played at the orphanage of Janusz Korczak and Stefa, conducted by the violinist, Abrasha.

The symphony ended. After the group of musicians, children went up to audition for the main role, among them the boy Abrasha had seen before sitting so nervously on his chair. "The little actor," as Abrasha called him in his heart.

The next morning, everyone hurried to the notice board

to see the list of actors for the Hanukkah play. Abrasha took his time, not hurrying with everyone else. He knew what would be on the board, he knew he himself would play a musical role this time, and he also knew that Korczak would not disappoint and that the new boy, whose acting ability was obvious, would receive the main role. From a distance, Abrasha could already see the boy with the "face of an actor" standing quite still for a moment in front of the notice board, before bursting into joyful cartwheels along the corridor. Abrasha laughed out loud.

THE STUDIO

After breakfast, the children went to the "store." The store was a little room at the end of the large hall in the orphanage, where the office equipment was kept: notebooks, erasers, pencils and crayons, and other writing utensils. Stefa was responsible for running the store. She stood waiting for her young clients, who used to come after breakfast for their equipment.

Yitzhak, or Yitzhakal'eh, as they used to call him, was the artist in the home. He always had a pencil stub in his hand, and took every opportunity to sit and fill whole notebooks with illustrations and sketches. That day, his notebook was full and there wasn't even space for one more picture. In order to receive another notebook, the children had to show Stefa the previous one, and only when she saw that the old notebook was indeed brimful, would she give out a new notebook in its place. Stefa wouldn't even exchange an old pencil stub that could still be used for a new pencil unless it could not be sharpened further. Only then would she exchange it.

Yitzhak took his old notebook from his personal drawer (each child had a personal drawer where they could keep all of their treasures). Yitzhak's drawer was full of treasures. There was a special marble, a piece of colored glass, a small stone, chestnuts he would play with, and his old notebook, which was ready to be replaced.

He ran to the "store," stood before Stefa, and held out his notebook. Stefa, who knew that ten-year-old Yitzhak was very talented at drawing, received him with a smile and asked: "You've finished another notebook?" You haven't skipped any pages? You learn so much? I gave you a new notebook only two days ago!" She took the notebook to check it, knowing in her heart that she'd find illustrations and sketches in there and not school material.

Stefa and Korczak encouraged the children to take an active interest in materials that attracted them. Stefa added: "I know you love drawing, so I have a suggestion for you: Please, take paper, paint brushes, and colored pencils and, whenever you want to paint, you can go to the secretary, take the key to the "store," and you can sit and paint here undisturbed."

Yitzhak was overjoyed, he felt his dream of becoming a painter was fulfilled. He felt proud because he knew that the suggestion originated from both Korczak and Stefa and if among all 107 children, they'd decided to invest in him, it meant he had a talent for drawing. Taking a deep breath, he thanked Stefa politely. Then he went outside and gave a great roar that echoed through the home. All those standing around him didn't understand what had happened, what mischief had he gotten into now?

The next day, Yitzhaka'leh went to the secretary and took the key to the store. When he got to the door, he realized that he barely reached the keyhole. He stood on the tips of his toes and opened the door. The room was small, but at that moment, it seemed to Yitzhak like a huge mansion. He spread the paper on the floor, took out his paintbrushes and colors, and got to work. He was so excited he had difficulty controlling himself.

He painted like the wind and when he was done, he looked at his work and his eyes darkened. It wasn't at all what he'd intended. He ripped up the paper, took a new sheet, again sketched several things, and again threw it into the bin. He did this several times until he began to feel miserable and frustrated. Suddenly, he remembered the breathing exercises Korczak had taught him, so he'd know how to calm himself when he was upset. He usually used these exercises when he was about to burst out at teachers in school or before a fight with another child. Now they served him there in the store, his painting "studio." "Breathe in and out slowly, only through the nose. Inhale through the nose and exhale slowly, calmly. Count ten breaths," Yitzhak heard Korczak's voice in his heart.

In and out through the nose he breathed, counting ten times, and once he'd calmed down, he stood before the sheet of paper and thought. He began to paint a landscape. The first brush strokes were hesitant, but after a few minutes he was in control of the technique and his imagination led him into mysterious realms. He painted landscapes, trees, and blue skies, and, of course, Warsaw's beloved Wisła River. The world he painted was beautiful. His paintings reflected the optimism and joy he'd acquired at the orphanage.

After a few days, he began to bring books he'd borrowed from the library to the "studio" and he'd sit and read there. He enjoyed the privacy and quiet in the little room when he was alone there. In time, Yitzhak felt that there, alone, he was learning to know himself. Gradually, he got to know the real Yitzhak. His thoughts and feelings. He began to love himself more, and his nature began to settle there, in the little room.

Nobody came to see what Yitzhak was doing in the little room on his own or what he was painting, not even Korczak or Stefa. They completely trusted him, which made him try harder and harder to improve.

Early one Friday morning, Stefa, the children's "tough mother," woke up and thought to herself: "It's a short day today and there's a lot of work to be done." She had to prepare the products for the Sabbath meal, order food, and cleaning materials, make sure that everyone's festive clothes had been laundered and ironed and were ready for the Sabbath, and see how many counselors would come to work that day. She looked at the long list of tasks before her and, sitting heavily down on the bed, thought: "Stefa, this is no time for self-indulgence. Get up now!" Suddenly, she heard a sound. She saw a sheet of paper being pushed under her door. On the large sheet was written in childish letters: *"Happy Birthday,"* underneath which was the painting of a woman.

"Who is that woman?" Stefa wondered to herself. She gazed at the benevolent eyes and gentle face reflected from the sheet. Her eyes again flickered over the Birthday blessing at the top of the sheet. "Why, today is my birthday!" Then she noticed something else on the face of the woman in the painting – a mole! The same familiar mole on her own face she used to joke about with the children: "The mole on my face is there to support the spectacles on my nose," she used to say.

Stefa was suddenly overcome with emotion as if she was about to weep. Is this how the children saw her? Here she is, painted on the sheet of paper: A beautiful, good-hearted woman, with black curious eyes, a generous mouth, a high wise forehead, and laughter lines on her face. Stefa embraced the painting and placed it for safekeeping on the shelf above her bed.

All morning, while working in the kitchen and laundry, the children could hear Stefa's voice singing cheerfully through the home. She did indeed have a happy birthday.

31 GIFTS

At the orphanage, they celebrated all Jewish holidays. Although Korczak himself was not a religious person, he believed that all the children had the right to maintain their beliefs and the traditional holidays they'd celebrated at home with their families. Thus, they celebrated all Jewish holidays according to tradition and the Shabbat, too, was a different and unique day.

From Friday morning onward, a special atmosphere prevailed in the home. Everyone was busy preparing for the Sabbath: baking challah bread, special cookies, and festive dishes. All the children would bathe and dress up for Friday night. On Saturday, they'd visit their families in the afternoon. The children would not go empty handed but would take their families some of the sweet pastries they'd prepared.

Those who didn't have a family stayed home with Korczak and Stefa. On these Saturdays, Stefa was proud to act as mother for the children who stayed home, having no one to visit.

Tamcza, a mischievous girl with long wild hair, who was liked by all the children, was constantly running from one place to another. Yulek was her best friend and was her exact opposite. A thoughtful boy, he was quiet and pleasant. Recently, Yulek had been troubled, and though Tamcza tried to find out why, he rejected her questions and withdrew into himself.

One Friday morning at the orphanage, the children noticed something odd: They saw Yulek surreptitiously inserting something in a packet and putting it into his bag. "Yulek, what have you got there?" They asked him and he ignored them. As if he hadn't heard the question. The children began to wonder if Yulek was stealing things from the orphanage, though nothing was missing. It was very strange. One hour went by and then another. The children gathered and followed Yulek. No one managed to see what he had in the small packets he kept putting in his bag.

Towards noon, Tamcza decided she had to decipher the mystery before the Sabbath began. What was Yulek taking from the home? "Home" was what everyone called the orphanage that was home to all the children. They all felt that what Yulek was stealing belonged to them as well and they were very troubled.

A group of children was making sandwiches with Stefa for everyone, several girls who had kitchen duty were making huge trays of the poppy seed cookies that the children loved, while others had cleaning chores, or were getting games ready for the evening. Korczak noticed that

Tamcza, usually daring and mischievous, was quieter than usual. She was unaware of Korczak's gaze because her eyes were constantly following Yulek. Korczak gazed at her, trying to understand the quiet tension enveloping her.

He called her and asked: Tamcza, is everything all right? Are you feeling well?"

"I'm fine," she nodded, her eyes continuing to follow Yulek.

"Tamcza, please go and see if the girls need help making cookies," Korczak told her, not understanding the meaning of her strange behavior.

Tamcza couldn't refuse the doctor's request and went to help the girls. From the corner of her eye, she noticed Yulek creeping into his room again, a small, white, creased cloth in his hand, which he put in his pocket. "What did he have there? Why was he going to his room every hour?" She wondered.

The moment her chore was finished, Tamcza quietly went up to the boys' dormitory and was just in time to see Yulek putting the white cloth into his bag. She found a hiding place and, the moment Yulek left the dormitory, she went inside, approached his bed, and opened his bag, whereupon her eyes opened in surprise. Tamcza closed his bag and put it back in its place. She went back down to the large hall and, her face red, she continued to help the girls make the tasty poppy seed cookies for the Sabbath.

The following day, the children went off to visit their families. Some of them had families in Warsaw who were forced to give up their children because they were poor. Some of the children had lost a mother or a father, and the remaining parent knew their child would receive a better education at Janusz Korczak's famous orphanage than at home.

Tamcza also came from a poor family. On Saturday, she went to visit her family in their modest home. She was playing with her younger brother, Pavel, when he suddenly said in his gentle voice: "Tamcza, didn't you bring us cookies today."

"I didn't have time to prepare any, I'll bring you some next time I come," she replied. "Come on, Pavel, let's play Lotto. I'm sure you'll beat me today," and he hurried after her.

At the same time, Yulek arrived at his family's home. His mother, Hannah, was celebrating her 30th birthday, and Yulek had wondered all week how to make her happy. He had no money for a gift. What could he bring her? Just something small to make her smile! His mother, the sole breadwinner, worked hard from morning till night. She cleaned houses, mended clothes for the neighbors, and took in washing for anyone who asked. All this to feed her ten children. Yesterday, on Friday morning, he'd woken to the wonderful smell of baking. He suddenly had an idea. Yes!

When he got home, in front of ten little siblings, he took from his bag the white cloths with everything he'd collected the entire morning. Every Friday he came to his mother's home with some of the Sabbath baking and shared it with his siblings, but to his astonishment, this time the hoard was even greater than he'd thought – 31 poppy seed cookies! A cookie for each year of her life and one more for the coming year. There was such excitement in the little house when his mother counted the cookies that matched her age in number. "How come you managed to bring so many cookies, my dearest boy? Thank you very much!" His mother was moved. His little brothers looked at her in alarm and calmed down when they realized that the tears they saw in her eyes were tears of joy. Yulek didn't understand how come there were 31 cookies in his bag.

When the Shabbat came to an end and they had all gathered once again at the orphanage, Yulek asked to speak privately to Doctor Korczak and, moved, told him what had happened. Korczak listened to Yulek, suddenly realizing the meaning of all the whispering of the children the day before, whenever Yulek passed by. The meaning of Tamcza's strange behavior. "You have good friends," said the doctor to Yulek. "You seem to be as good a friend to them too."

The following day, on Sunday morning, when they were all standing in line for the daily dose of disgusting fish oil, Tamcza held her nose, closed her eyes tight, and opened her mouth to receive from Korczak the piece of bread with salt he gave her every day. Suddenly, on her tongue, she felt the wonderful taste of a sweet poppy seed cookie. Surprised, she opened one eye and saw Korczak wink at her, as if saying without words: "You're a wonderful little girl!" And indeed, she did feel wonderful.

A DANGEROUS
ADVENTURE AT THE
WISŁA RIVER

"Kuba, Shmulik, come quickly. We're late, Igor is waiting downstairs for us!" Shouted Kobush, as he slid down the banister and ran in the direction of the carpentry shop.

Igor was Korczak's helper. He enjoyed sculpting objects and animals out of wood. It was his one serious hobby and the children persuaded him to start a handicraft class.

For some weeks, the boys had been building a kayak in the handicrafts classroom. They met in the carpentry workshop and worked hard. They carved, polished, and sawed, listening to the instructions of Igor and Felek, his assistant. The children knew he'd once been a kayak champion and adored him, receiving all of the advice he gave them during the construction. Slowly, the kayak emerged: Majestic and elegant, as if it had been there all along, just waiting to have the excess wood sculpted away.

The boys dreamed of paddling their kayak on the Wisła, the river that crossed Warsaw, accessible from every point. For years they'd been listening to the stories Korczak told them. They wanted to sail off into their own adventure. They imagined sailing to a distant country, like the characters in the stories they heard. To find valuable treasure and save their friends and families from a life of poverty. Their hands were bruised and callused from sanding the wood, but their eyes shone with excitement while they worked long hours in the carpentry shop.

"Boys, you must name the kayak," said counselor Felek with great seriousness.

"We'll call it Cheeby in honor of that movie we saw." Suggested Kuba, the poet in the group. They all nodded in agreement. "Cheeby the Kayak" sounds perfect, as if it had been created during the six days of Genesis.

Slowly but surely, Cheeby the Kayak became as smooth as silk, and they all knew the time was coming when they'd take Cheeby to the river and launch her. And indeed, one day, Igor said proudly: "Friends, we're done! Go up to eat and sleep and tomorrow, Friday afternoon, we will all take Cheeby out on her maiden voyage." The cheerful, proud friends did as their teachers told them and went noisily upstairs.

The following day was sunny and pleasant. The children walked in a cheerful line towards the River Wisła, carrying paddles in their hands. They sang the entire way. Korczak, Igor, the teacher, and counselor, Felek, led the group, and they were joined by all the children who came to cheer on the three brave kayak paddlers.

The gray water sparkled as if hinting to the children: "This is no joke, friends, it's our domain. We flow quietly and peacefully, but beware and take care!"

The children knew the river well with its calm waters, gray color, and peace, and they all knew how to swim. After all, every summer they'd go down to the River Wisła to play, fool around and practice swimming.

Suddenly they heard Korczak's voice, almost in prayer: *"Gray Wisła, I love your banks covered with the wetland shrubs reflected within you. I love your sands and the stars that bathe in your waters."*

"Good luck, Cheeby," said Igor. He thumped the boys encouragingly on their shoulders and lovingly stroked the kayak. "Off you go!"

The water was quiet and mirror-like. Counselor Felek, together with Kobush and Shmulik, the young builders, held the kayak, balancing themselves while holding tightly to the wetland shrubs growing in the shallows. Carefully, they lowered the kayak into the water, got in, and began to paddle down river.

"Friends, paddle to the right! Hey, Kobush, now left...no, no! Shmulik, you're not with us!" The children on the bank could hear Igor's helper, Felek, shouting and suddenly, he didn't seem such an expert on sailing. Slowly the kayak was carried towards the bridge, where there were heavy concrete columns. Igor realized what was about to happen to Cheeby their Kayak that they'd worked so hard to build. He stripped off his shirt and hurriedly got into the water.

"Right, not left! Right! Kobuuush...!

Boom! A loud thump was heard and everyone watched Cheeby the Kayak, break in two. Two pieces of wood floated away on the Wisła, each one in a different direction. The pieces of wood swiftly disappeared down the river, as if Cheeby had never existed. The children stood on the banks of the river and gazed with incredulity. They watched the disappointed paddlers who had started to swim back to shore.

Korczak and Igor gathered the distressed children together and, to everyone's surprise, Korczak pulled out the story about "Kaitush the Wizard" and began to read it to the children:

Again about the Wisła and the wooden houses along the bank, the fishermen's huts. Added to them were farms and castles. The murmuring of the evergreen forests could still be heard, but the tall trees were dwindling away on the banks of the gray river. Eons and eons ago... The ancient Wisła...flowed from the mountains to the sea. At a certain point of the broad flow was my town. My river. Me."

Everyone's eyes shone with excitement. Cheeby the Kayak merged in the children's hearts, together with the strong, ancient river in the story of Kaytek, a Polish child who, like each of the children now standing on the riverbank, eyes bright with excitement, felt how many adventures still lay in store.

THE KITE GIRL

All the children sat at the table, focusing on their work. They were trying to make their kites more beautiful, larger, and more colorful. Mostly the boys liked making kites, but so did Dvorka and a new, younger girl called Flonya.

Flonya had arrived at the orphanage without a family. She'd been found wandering the streets, ill, thin, and abandoned. Despite all the doctor's attempts to get her to talk, Flonya said not a word. Korczak's concern for the girl was apparent. He'd occasionally examine her and make notes in his journal. He measured her height, the circumference of her skull, and her weight. While doing so, he'd attempt to amuse her and, once, almost succeeded. Korczak told some joke, and suddenly Flonya's eyes began to shine and though she almost smiled, she immediately tightly closed her mouth and returned to her usual sad expression.

Only in the workshop was Flonya completely different. She always tried to finish her chores swiftly and be the first to reach the workshop, waiting at the doorway until the counselor arrived. As she built her kites, her face was calm and peaceful. On the table were thin, hollow, bamboo canes, scissors and colored crepe paper, bowls of glue made from flour, as well as crayons, string and copy paper. In short, everything necessary to prepare the perfect kite. Korczak would explain to the children, especially the younger ones, how to build a kite. He would help anyone who asked for help and also make himself a small, simple kite.

Flonya would come to the workshop without a sketch and immediately begin to draw and cut precisely, as if she had a plan ready in her mind. Using copy paper, she'd accurately copy the sketch lines on the back of the kite. From one visit to the next, the silent little girl's kite progressed. The work continued for several weeks and, every week, Flonya chose different colors. One side of the kite was dark and serious, but she painted the other side of the kite with a mass of colors. The doctor was moved when he saw the wonderful brightness. He sat down beside her, working on his own kite.

Flonya always worked in silence, but Korczak wasn't deterred. He persevered, talking to her, telling her stories and asking her questions without expecting an answer. One day, when Flonya's kite was already decorated with a myriad of colors, a thin, unfamiliar voice was heard in the workshop, addressing Dvorka: "Would you pass me that little stick. I want to make a tail out of it for my kite."

The children stopped working and looked up in amazement. Even Korczak turned around, but didn't interfere in the conversation between the girls. "Here you are," replied

Dvorka casually. "Come on, I'll help you," and both continued to work together on Flonya's kite. The girls' kite was large, colorful and the most sophisticated in the workshop. Dvorka, who was experienced, having already built several kites, helped her new friend. The more the building of the kite progressed, the more relaxed Flonya became.

And then came the moment to tie the tail to the kite. There were many kinds of string: thick, fine, smooth and curly, but Flonya chose the finest string on the table. Each stage of building the kite was noted in Korczak's curious mind. He wrote down everything in his journal. He observed and interpreted the improvement in Flonya's behavior, like a pediatrician exploring the child's psyche in action.

The day came for the children to go out and fly their kites. They stood in a line, some holding a large kite, others a small one. There were kites in all kinds of colors, kites in the shape of an animal, or a monster, each one according to the richness of their imagination and the wonder of their creation. When the signal was given, they all broke into a run up the hill. The kites began to fly upward, higher and higher. It was an entrancing and colorful sight. The warm sun and the wind that morning heralded a wonderful day for kite flying.

Flonya ran beside her new friend, Dvorka. One girl was slight, serious, and thin, the other tall and cheerful with legs like a deer. Both were laughing and happy. Their charming kite was attached to a fine string and navigated by Flonya's small hand.

Korczak observed the girls. He gazed at Flonya and noticed her internal struggle: Something inside her longed to free the kite, but something else in her wanted to go on navigating it because she had become attached to it. She'd never had a game of her own before. She held tight to the string, unable to free the kite.

Korczak put his hand over Flonya's small one. She sensed the warmth of his hand, felt secure, peaceful, and... she released the large kite into the sky. The kite climbed swiftly upward as if enjoying its sudden liberation, Flonya feeling the same.

THE SWEET SCENT
OF HOME

Little Stashek suffered from insomnia. When everyone else was already asleep, he was still staring at the ceiling. When he did fall asleep, he was awakened by bad dreams. Sometimes he cried, sometimes he even woke and found he'd wet himself.

One Thursday, Korczak returned late from the newspaper where he worked. Just as he entered the building, Stashek woke in alarm. The boys around him were fast asleep but Stashek was convinced that he'd heard something. The approach of quiet steps. He tried to work out what those sounds were and then noticed something else: He smelled the scent of warm, fresh bread that had recently been baked. Out of the corner of his eye he saw Korczak going quietly from one bed to another and placing something under the pillow of each child. Stashek sat up in bed. Was he dreaming again?

"Shh...Shh..." Korczak gestured with his finger, "Quiet!"

When he reached Stashek's bed he gave him a piece of Turkish bread with raisins and signaled to him to eat it quietly. "Make sure there aren't any crumbs on your bed, or Stefa will shout at me," whispered Korczak and winked at him. He continued to break the bread into small pieces, putting them under the pillow of each child in the large dormitory.

There was a rule in the orphanage: It was forbidden to eat in the dormitories. It was especially forbidden to eat in bed, but Korczak was a rascal. He'd frequently behave like one of the children. Stashek slowly chewed the sweet bread, enjoying each bite. The bread had a special taste, the taste of a prank.

Stashek felt he was partner to a secret and felt proud that of all the children, only he was awake at night with Korczak. The next night Stashek lay in bed, again expecting Korczak. He lay daydreaming and, for the first time since he'd arrived at the orphanage, he drifted off and slept without nightmares. He dreamed the doctor came to him and, in his hand, was a whole loaf of bread dotted with raisins like stars in the sky. He hummed to himself in the dream and suddenly awoke, without knowing why.

Stashek sat up in bed. Around him fifty boys were fast asleep. Some changed their position, someone snored, and Stashek looked hopefully at the door. Precisely what he hoped would happen actually did! The doctor came in again, this time carrying tiny parcels in his hand. He walked quietly to Josef's bed and put something under his pillow, and then he approached little Stashek's bed. He put something under his pillow too. Korczak gave Stashek a warm hug. "Awake again, Stashek? It's time you slept the whole night through. You're a big boy after all. You have a birthday tomorrow. You're eight years old," added the doctor.

Eight years old! Stashek was very excited. He hadn't known his birth date. It was some years since anyone had related to this date and nobody had ever celebrated it with him. Now, in his new home at the orphanage, they'd celebrate his birthday. Stashek looked into the doctor's good eyes and went back to sleep.

That night, the fragrance of the package Korczak had put under Stashek's pillow filled his dreams. It was the wonderful smell of the birthday cake his mother had baked for him. Once. A long time ago.

From that night on, Stashek no longer suffered from insomnia or nightmares. He sometimes had difficulty getting up in the morning, as befits an eight-year-old boy who wants just one more minute to enjoy his sweet dreams.

APRIL LOVE

The children had spent the whole day preparing gear for the trip they'd be going on early the following day. The girls' dormitory was quiet, everyone was asleep. Only Gutcza, the prettiest girl in the orphanage, was awake. Daydreaming, she lay in bed. Gutcza was dreaming about Barry, the handsome boy who'd arrived at the orphanage a month earlier. His black hair was so thick, her hand almost stretched out to stroke it.

His green eyes occasionally stared shamelessly at her, his long neck stiffening with curiosity and his mouth seemed to say, wordlessly: "How beautiful you are."

A thoughtful, healthy girl, always in control of her emotions, Gutcza didn't understand why she was so preoccupied with Barry. She thought to herself: "I just like Barry, of course I'm not in love with him. It's probably just because today is the first day of spring and I'm in a romantic mood."

Gutcza remembered how she'd sat that morning in the yard and plucked petals from a fragrant white flower. Loves me, loves me not. Loves me, loves me not. When the last petal in her hand indicated "loves me not," she was very sad. Korczak sat next to her. He was very familiar with the game "Loves me, loves me not", and knew that the person playing the game says these words while plucking one petal after another. Only the last petal determines if the person loves you or not.

Korczak saw Gutcza's face fall when the last petal left in her hand meant "loves me not", and caught the expression of sadness that spread over her face. He went to her and said quietly: "Gutczinka, he likes you a lot! He simply doesn't want the boys to laugh at him, so he ignores you. Don't be sad, I know everything will turn out alright." Gutcza opened her eyes, not knowing how the doctor knew everything, even her innermost thoughts.

Now, in bed in the dormitory, Gutcza remembered what Korczak had said to her that morning in the yard. Slowly, she cheered up. If the doctor had guessed how she felt, could it be a sign he'd guessed right, even regarding Barry's feelings for her? She smiled to herself, her eyes closed and she fell asleep.

The beginning of spring was always accompanied by a sense of renewal at the home. That morning everyone woke up feeling excited. They hurried to get up and get ready, they slid down the banister on their way to the dining room, smiling at each other and laughing during breakfast. They'd soon be off on their short trip. They could even imagine how many good experiences they'd have on the first spring trip. After breakfast, they were about to set off quickly, their hats on their heads, when they suddenly heard Korczak's voice: "Who has green? Who has green on the first day of spring?" And Barry was the first to pull a green leaf from his pocket. "Good for you, you deserve a candy from me!" The doctor told him.

Korczak enjoyed surprising the children with the game "Who has green?" He stopped the children on all kinds of occasions, suddenly asking them: "Who has green?" Whoever had something green in their pocket received a small gift from Korczak. The children always had a green leaf in their pockets, green paper, or anything else the color green, because they knew the doctor would surprise them and they wanted to win the game. The prize may only have been a candy, but winning was sweeter than candy.

The children paired off, Korczak made sure they had all their gear and gave final instructions to the counselors. They took a route along the river. The weather warmed up slightly. Korczak strode at the head of the line, deep in thought.

"Who would like my candy?" Asked Barry and looked at Gutcza, hoping she'd say something. Before Gutcza had time to say a word, Rocha'leh jumped forward and took the candy. "Me! Me! I said first."

Barry was disappointed but didn't say a word. He looked away at the flowers blooming at the side of the path. The sight soothed him. He walked beside Gutcza, sensing she, too, was calm and happy. There's nothing like good weather, blue skies, and a pleasant, tranquil breeze.

Bees, beetles, and butterflies flew briskly among the

flowers, and many birds were seen in the sky. A herd of cows was grazing and Korczak, who was leading the children, suddenly said in a cheerful voice: "You're my herd. Mooo, mooo!"

The children constantly asked questions. "Why do we have to wear tall boots?" "Why are there so many butterflies now?" "Where are all those lines of ants going?" Korczak answered all the questions while they took a brief water break. He made sure everyone drank water and rested.

"Hey Henryk, why are you covering the ants with soil?" Called the doctor loudly, immediately softening and explaining to the boy the consequences of his rash action. "Henryk, you are bothering those ants at their labor and torturing them. Why did you pour soil on them? What have they done to you? Ants are hardworking creatures. Think about it: Every morning, at dawn when it's cold outside, they leave the nest in search of food. They hoard food for the winter when it's cold and wet and snow covers everything and it's impossible to find food. Ants are social creatures and what are you doing, crushing them with sand?" Henryk reddened and said: "I'm sorry, I didn't know. I was just playing with sand and didn't notice." Korczak smiled, he imagined that not one child would now want to hurt the tiny creatures.

After drinking and resting, they prepared to continue their walk, when Korczak asked: "Children, before we go on – are there any more questions?"

"Yes," said Ludvika in a loud voice. "Can a frog catch a cold?"

Everyone burst out laughing, but Korczak replied seriously: "The frog belongs to the amphibian family. Like humans, it also has a respiratory system and so it can catch a cold," then he added laughingly that "it can also sneeze."

The children began to make jokes. "Can it also hiccough? Fart?"

They all laughed for some time. Gutcza sat opposite Barry. They exchanged glances from time to time. She decided to be as brave as he was and not look away. Who will look away first, she said to herself. So they sat there, ignoring the children's giggles, staring at each other.

After a while, Korczak looked at his watch and said: "Children, up you get! We're continuing our walk." Everyone got up. Quite naturally and without thinking much about it, Barry held out a hand to Gutcza. She took his outstretched hand, got up, and they continued to walk, her hand remaining in his.

"I suppose frogs fall in love too," said Sholem, who was Barry's best friend and a little jealous now, realizing that his friend had been taken away from him. And for what? Love?

"Watch your step!" said Korczak. "In the spring season, snakes come out of their hiding places and they're extremely dangerous! They're very hungry when they emerge from hibernation. If you cross their path, they will bite you. You, too, Sholem, bite your tongue!" Korczak said seriously, but as he spoke, he gave the jealous little Sholem, a small wink.

The hikers arrived at their destination: A curve in the river that formed a large area surrounded by trees and flowers. The perfect place to play and rest. They all removed their backpacks and sat down to eat the tasty sandwiches they'd brought from home. The couple in love found themselves a secluded place under an old oak tree. Barry took out his penknife and began to carve the name of his beloved into the bark. When everyone had finished their meal, they played football and catch for a while, and wandered happily along the riverbank.

On the way home, Korczak glanced at the couple in love who were walking together at the end of the line. The flowers that had begun to bloom were a perfect background for the two children. Black-haired Barry with his green eyes and Gutcza, the prettiest girl in the home, walking hand in hand, a rearguard for the group of children.

Korczak and his colleague, Stefa, had so often witnessed youth's first love, new and blossoming in front of their eyes, and they never tired of gazing at this pure love. He was glad to see these two wonderful children joining the ranks of boys and girls joyfully in love - and on the first day of spring too.

The group returned to the orphanage. Not one child had gotten lost, or been bitten by a snake, and not one child would ever again pour sand on ants. Everyone now knew that frogs could catch a cold, and that spring was excellent for lovers.

IN THE FAIRY TALE
FOREST

The forest looked as if it had come out of a fairy tale. Fir trees stretched out huge branches in all directions and strange shapes were formed by the twisted trunks of the pine trees. A rustling wind played in the treetops, through whose branches peeped a scrap of sky and a stray cloud. Summer flowers were blooming, birds were chirping, and in the midst of all this was a tiny, round forest clearing where a small boy was lying.

Hinda lay on his back, a green stem in his mouth. He stared up at the blue sky, the sunrays touching the trees, and the play of light and shade on the leaves as they moved in the wind. He felt a bit cold there in the forest. He wore a scarf around his neck but his clothes were thin, shabby, and dirty, and his shoes were torn.

Bored, he'd wandered the forest that day and found no

friends, even the bees were busy gathering food for the cold days to come. He lay watching them fly from one flower to another, buzzing as if to bless the visitor.

For several months now he'd leave the village every morning, bored and wandering alone. He'd discovered the fairy tale forest on one of his outings. His parents were dead, and he'd recently moved to live with a distant aunt in a tiny village. His aunt worked most of the day and paid scant attention to him. In remote villages at the time, adults worked hard and young children didn't always go to school but helped make a living. It would be hard to say that he felt welcome in his aunt's home, but he felt good in the forest. He had food and water; the trees were his friends and the sunrays made him happy.

The sun beat down on his face and he lay with closed eyes under the branches of a young pine tree, listening to the sounds of the forest. "What was that?" He thought to himself when he heard children's voices. "Am I dreaming?" He jumped up and, light as a monkey, climbed into the treetop.

Underneath him was a group of children and, leading them was a man with an orange beard and round spectacles who, from time to time, bent over one of the children and quietly explained something to him. Hinda couldn't hear what he said but the man's voice was very quiet. Suddenly, the children's commotion ceased and everyone bent over and looked at the ground. In the prevailing quiet, Hinda could hear the man's words.

"You see, children, those are the feathers of a pygmy warbler, a tiny bird that lives in forests. It is very hard to find, but we'll try. It usually looks for the nests of other birds and takes them over. If we're quiet, we might manage to find it."

"Hey, I know where the bird is," shouted Hinda.

Astonished, everyone looked at the boy who was swiftly sliding down the tree.

"Hello, my friend," said the adult. He approached the boy and laid a warm hand on his head. He was calm, as if a child falling from the sky in the heart of the forest was an ordinary event.

"Pleased to meet you, my name is Janusz Korczak," the man introduced himself to Hinda.

"I'm Hinda," he replied. "I visit the forest every day and know all the animals here. They're my friends."

"What are you doing here alone in the forest?" Asked one of the girls.

Although Hinda had only just met Korczak and the group of children, he felt so comfortable in their company that he began to tell them in his high voice: "My poor aunt, things are so hard for her. She's alone and the work is very hard. She doesn't have the time to cook me meals, or keep an eye on me and what I'm doing, and I don't want to be a burden to her. So I decided to leave home and every day I wander along the paths. That's how I got to the forest. I feel good here in the forest, I have friends like the trees and the flowers, the birds, the wind and the sun, it's good here. But who are you?" He remembered to ask. "Why have you come here?"

Korczak listened attentively to Hinda. It was clear that the things he heard pained him. He said to the boy: "This is

Yitzchak'aleh, Sophie, Basha, Semek, Shlomo..." He named all the children. "We all live together in a large home in Warsaw and come here every summer on holiday," said Korczak, pointing in the direction of the summer huts at the entrance to the forest. "Actually, we were looking for a talented, knowledgeable boy like you who knows the forest. Would you like to join us? Spend time, learn and live with us for the coming month while we're here."

"I'll meet your aunt, talk to her and see if she'll agree to your joining us for the summer vacation and you can stay with us until we have to return to the city," added Korczak. "The children will vote to decide whether or not you can stay with us in the forest."

Hinda had already forgotten how pleasant it was to have someone take care of him. He looked into Korczak's blue eyes, seeing only love reflected there. Such kind eyes, that accepted him with devotion, without conditions or questions.

He looked at the children again, expecting to find derision, laughter, or pity in their eyes, but to his astonishment, he saw all of them regarding him with joy and even understanding. He suddenly thought that maybe they too had known the loneliness, sadness, and lack of trust he was feeling at that moment.

The group of children took Hinda in as naturally as their teacher had – with unconditional love. Korczak suddenly said to the children: "It seems to me that you should thank Hinda for wanting to join our children's group. We, the city children, will learn from him about life in the forest. What a gift!"

"I can hear it..." Hinda interrupted him. Everyone, the children and Korczak, fell silent. From one of the bushes came a rustling sound, and there was the warbling pygmy in all its splendor, standing among the bushes and looking at them innocently.

"Children, it's a miracle! It's not every day we see a bird like that," whispered Korczak excitedly. His shining eyes noticed a gray feather that had fallen on the ground. He picked it up.

Hinda felt a miracle had happened to him, too, in finding his own "new flock." Just as the wolves in the forest live in packs, monkeys live in troupes, the trees have a community and, in the same way, everything in the world has meaning.

He hoped his aunt would be happy for him to join this large group of children because, her love for him notwithstanding, she found it hard to raise him. Despite this, he was already missing her and hoped that his aunt would be able to visit him sometimes and that they'd stay in touch through letters.

All the children got in line and began to go back in the direction of the farm where they stayed in the summer. The name of the farm towards which they were walking, accompanied by Hinda, was "Rozyczka." The farm had been donated to the orphanage by a Warsaw Jew called Cohen, whose beloved, only daughter Rozya, had died in childhood.

Hinda wondered to himself: "What will this place look like?" He felt he'd reached a safe place.

THE FEATHER OF THE WARBLING PYGMY

The Rozyczka Farm consisted of several huts arranged in a U-shape, with a pretty, nurtured garden where tomato and cucumber plants burst out of the earth. Herbs were carefully arranged in planters, with an equal space between each plant so that they could grow under good conditions.

Yunus had come to the orphanage the previous month. Korczak had hesitated about taking him to camp with everyone because he didn't know all the house rules yet and Korczak wasn't sure it would be good for him to go to camp before he had properly adjusted. In the end, he decided to include him in the summer vacation so as not to distress him.

When Yunus saw the nurtured vegetable garden on the farm, his first thought was that if he didn't like it there and wanted to leave, he could creep into the vegetable garden, fill his pockets with vegetables and fruit and escape. Thus, he'd go back to the street with his pockets full and not empty-handed. At that moment, Yunus had just returned with all the children from a walk in the fairy forest, he crossed the pretty vegetable garden and they all got ready for a meal.

A few days previously, on a walk in the forest, the children had found the rare feather of a warbling pygmy. Excited by the special find, Korczak described the life of this bird: "Well, children, the warbling pygmy is a kind of night bird from the owl family. Its head is large and broad, its eyes are in the front of the head and protrude, which gives it an extraordinary range of vision. Its neck is long and flexible so it can turn its head 270 degrees. The warbling pygmy isn't usually active during the day, so it really is a stroke of luck to have found it."

When they returned to camp, Korczak placed the special feather inside the book on the table, the book he read to the children every evening. So the feather became a bookmark. Yunus would have preferred to stick it in his hair, like the feather of an ancient king. Yunus had a rich collection of 78 feathers, but this unique feather was not one of them.

After the meal, Yunus wandered about the huts, examining each object, browsing through the books and newspapers in every corner. He saw so many things around him that he would like to take and put in his backpack. Could he take food in his pockets? Maybe swipe some fruit standing on the table outside the cooler?

Since the day the warbling pygmy's feather was found, he wanted more than anything to take it and put it in his backpack, without anyone seeing. The feather was rare, and he knew it. His eyes darted here and there with confusion and excitement, occasionally meeting the glance of the doctor (as he'd heard the children call him), who didn't seem to be looking at him at all, but nonetheless, his eyes soothed him. During the day, the children worked, played, organized, and prepared food. Yunus noticed that the hours passed and he didn't know if he was playing or working because everything was done peacefully and laughingly and, sometimes, with song. Every child knew exactly what they had to do. Nobody had to fight for anything here, there was enough food for everyone, and if they wanted more, it was given without anger or urgency. They simply asked and received with pleasure.

In the late afternoon, the children were given time to play. Yunus wandered thoughtfully among the groups of children. He had a hard time finding his place and choosing which group to join. He preferred being in the open air. He saw a group of children playing a game known as "bark." They beat on a small tree trunk and ran from one point to another in the yard. Yunus, whose head was whirling with everything going on, went to the games corner where he met Yitzchaka'leh, a small boy who stood painting with great seriousness on a canvas set on a wooden easel. It looked like a real painting. And there was also a small group of children who, instead of playing, gathered round the doctor and seemed to be waiting for something.

The doctor lifted the book and said: "Well, my friends, shall we go on reading our book? Where did we stop yesterday?" He opened the thick book and looked for the valuable feather he'd put there that morning. He looked and looked but couldn't find it.

The doctor glanced at Yunus and smiled at him with his good eyes. "Children, I remind you that Charles Dickens was a writer who wrote a lot about children. About their poverty and hardship, the orphanages where they suffered ill treatment, and he also wrote about their successes and their ability to overcome the harsh reality they were born into and achieve a good and enriching life. Now, I will continue to read to you from the book "Oliver Twist," remember?"

Korczak began to read. The children sat around him and listened. None of them suspected that something had happened, and Korczak's expression certainly didn't give away the fact that he knew who had taken the feather. Only Yunus felt his face redden and that at any minute he might burst with shame. Korczak continued to read in a pleasant voice, and Yunus gradually began to calm down.

The story was fascinating, and Yunus listened attentively to Korczak as he read in his dramatic voice:

"He rose from the table; and advancing to the master, basin and spoon in hand, said: somewhat alarmed at his own temerity: 'Please, sir, I want some more.'"

The master aimed a blow at Oliver's head with the ladle; pinioned him in his arm; and shrieked aloud for the beadle.

The board were sitting in solemn conclave, when Mr. Bumble rushed into the room in great excitement, and addressing the gentleman in the high chair, said,

'Mr. Limbkins, I beg your pardon, sir! Oliver Twist has asked for more!'

Yunus was swept away into another world, almost forgetting that very soon the book would be closed, and the doctor would probably tell him the time had come for him to leave because there was no place there for thieves. However, when Korczak closed the book, he merely said: "Good night, get ready for bed, we've had a long day full of adventures. Tomorrow another full day awaits us. We'll come to say good night in a while." He left the thick book on the table, approached Yunus, and said quietly: "Yunus, come and say good night to our mother – Miss Stefa."

Stefa, Korczak's colleague, rarely came to the summer camp. When everyone was at camp in the summer, she would prepare the home for the New Year. When all the children returned to Warsaw, suntanned after a month at camp, they'd find the home painted and renovated, clean and ready for them. And waiting at the door for them, they'd find a longing Stefa.

Stefa, as Korczak had said, was like a mother to the children. A strong woman who ran the home during all hours of the day. Without Stefa, Korczak would not have managed to run the place.

Stefa approached Yunus, held out a warm hand and said: "Come to bed, my child."

Her pleasant voice calmed Yunus' alarmed thoughts. He followed her to the boys' dormitory, to the bed nearest the door.

"Sweet dreams," said Stefa and covered him with a

blanket. A bold and stealthy plan took shape in Yunus' head. He pretended to be asleep. In the meantime, Stefa went to the girls' dormitory.

Korczak entered the boys' dormitory. As he usually did, he talked to the children who had difficulty falling asleep and soothed those who suffered from nightmares. On his way out, he approached Yunus who was lying in bed with his eyes closed and stroked his forehead, before he, too, went to the girls' dormitory.

Yunus opened his eyes, pulled back the blanket, and ran to the kitchen. Two minutes later, he returned to bed, this time falling asleep with a smile on his lips.

When Stefa and Korczak returned to the kitchen to rest after the labors of the day, they sat down with a cup of hot tea. "Look!" Stefa pointed proudly to the kitchen table. On the book lay the warbling pygmy's feather. Korczak didn't say a word, but his good eyes shone.

"You know," he said to Stefa, "there's no need to get mad at the boy, no need to shame him in front of others. The fact that we believe in him and respect him enables him to forgive himself."

"Here," he too pointed at the feather lying on the book. "Yunus resolved what he did by himself. I believe it's a sign that he trusts us. That's enough for me."

LANDSCAPER

In the last bed, right next to the door to the large dormitory, Natek was asleep. He was a very thin boy, the thinnest of the children. It was his first year at summer camp. His father had owned a large construction business in Warsaw and when his parents were killed in an accident the previous year, distant relatives brought him to be educated at Janusz Korczak's orphanage. Its name was well-known as an excellent educational institution throughout Poland.

Natek loved reading. He also liked sketching models and buildings, but he didn't participate in any kind of sport. He wasn't good at it. He woke in his bed in the camp hut, and it took him a moment to remember where he was. He sometimes felt quite lonely at camp.

Korczak came in as usual to wake the children. Most of the children were already up. Natek heard them planning their day together in groups in excited whispers: The children who loved running through the fields, the children who longed to go treasure hunting in the forest with Korczak, and the youths from the "big" group, who went out every day to work on the farm and were even paid for it. Natek had no one to whisper with. He turned over and dozed.

Right above his bed, a pair of eyes gazed at him through round spectacles. "What's up, Natek? Don't you feel well?" Doctor Korczak put a pleasant, dry, soft hand on Natek's forehead. "Are you ill?"

Natek was ashamed for worrying the doctor. "No, I'm just tired after yesterday's walk," he said, preparing to get up, but before he could sit up, Korczak's fingers stroked his forehead, as if he understood that the boy felt like he needed a little time alone, to stay in the pleasant bed and get special attention from Korczak. "You can stay and doze a little longer," said Korczak. "When you wake up, join us for breakfast."

Natek stayed cozily in bed for a few more minutes. He felt better in the quiet room without the children's commotion. Hearing everyone clearing the breakfast dishes and getting ready to go out for the various activities, he jumped out of bed and ran, calling out to the children: "Wait for me, wait for me!"

He joined the group of younger children. He was small for his age. They all ran barefoot to the dunes. Korczak accompanied this group that day. As usual, he walked slowly behind, deep in thought.

The children began to play in the sand. One built a castle, another dug a hole, a third sculpted imaginary animals and a fourth skipped barefoot along the deep, pleasant sand. They all seemed to be separate, but although Natek couldn't explain it to himself, he felt as if they were playing together.

He gazed around him and saw them building, dismantling, crumbling, and building again. He closed his eyes and remembered the days he'd sat with his father at the sketching table at their construction company. Together, they sat dreaming, planning, sketching, and, finally, they built too.

Natek felt profound shock, everything he'd tried to forget for a whole year burst out there, in the dunes, at Korczak's summer camp. He burst into tears. Sadness fell upon him like heavy sand, but underneath it, another emotion emerged – relief. Deep inside he knew that weeping was a good thing, the weeping of release. He went on watching the children, each one preoccupied, and he promised himself he'd no longer try to forget. The opposite, he'd be glad to remember. Forever. A loving memory of Mama and Papa.

"Hey, Natek," said Szymontek, who was sitting close by. Like all the children in the group who had gone to the dunes, Szymontek was younger than Natek but had been in the orphanage longer. From his expression, it was impossible to tell if he'd noticed Natek's storm of emotion. "Find a corner. The sand here is like the sand at the seashore!" "See what I'm doing," he explained with pride in his great creativity. "I always dig a deep wide hole, and then I invite a friend to spend time in the cool sand."

Natek began to design a unique hole, just as he remembered his father doing. With his small finger, he sketched the outlines of his plan in the sand, and only after he was done, he began to dig until he reached a depth of a meter and a half, maybe even more.

When he looked up, he saw more holes like that.

Some of the holes had been filled by the children. This is what Korczak had taught them: When you leave the hole, you must fill it up in case someone falls into it. Natek's eyes were swollen with weeping, his hands were red from the effort of digging and he was hungry, after all, he'd missed breakfast, but he felt good.

As the hours passed, so "togetherness" surpassed "solitude." The children had time to build wonderful imaginary things. They'd all created and built what they felt like and, gradually, they began to look around at their friends' creativity and to help one another. One received a shell from a friend because he didn't have one, and another received a leaf with a special shape. Various materials lay scattered around them like an abundant treasure, and each child used them according to their taste. Stones, plants, shells, everything served the art of sculpting, design, and landscaping.

All this time, Korczak sat on the side, humming an old childhood song to himself, and appeared to be enjoying himself watching his children at work, finding their creative path in the sand with the materials and with each other. Finally, he couldn't resist it and approached to praise the artwork. Sometimes, when they asked his advice, he'd help. When he reached Natek's hole, he asked: "Can I join you?" Natek was overjoyed at the attention. It was the second time that day! He immediately invited the doctor to enjoy his new "home."

"Are you feeling well?" Asked Korczak.

Natek replied: "I feel very well! Very well! I built the big hole according to a plan." He showed Korczak the sketched plan on the sand beside the hole. "I can always invite a friend to be here with me."

Korczak smiled at him, got up, and jumped out. "Come on, children, let's all look at what you've done, and then we'll return to the farm. You are probably thirsty. It's hot today."

Then Korczak introduced the sand artworks as if he were a guide at an exhibition. "Don't I always tell you that each child is unique? Well, so are your holes. Look at them: Each child has created something different, something special for himself."

And indeed, the children saw that each hole was different and special: one was deep, another wide, one had a special stone inserted and another was covered in green leaves. Together they examined the differences and, of course, were impressed by Natek's hole, and by the plan he'd sketched in advance.

"Before we fill the holes with sand, I want you to pay attention to the type of sandy earth here," said Korczak, who changed from being a guide at an art exhibition into a science teacher. "It's different from the red earth at the farm. Note the plants that grow here."

"Look!" cried a child who was looking at the earth as Korczak had suggested and discovered something. "You can see the special steps of every animal and insect in the sand." Together they sat analyzing all the "findings" they'd collected, like researchers of nature. When they were done, each child chose something to hide in his hole, something special like a beautiful stone or feather. Then they filled in the holes so that nobody would fall into them by mistake and got ready to return to the farm.

When they arrived at the farm, they found jugs of water, sandwiches, and fruit waiting on the table. Natek felt like leaping on the food. He approached the table quickly and put one hand out to the jug and another to a sandwich, and then he saw a notice above the table.

On the board in a handwriting that everyone recognized was written: *Help yourselves. Eat and drink, but make sure there's enough for your friends."* At once, Natek calmed down. He swallowed his saliva, stood in line and politely took a sandwich and glass of water. Only after everyone had helped themselves to food and drink, and everyone had eaten together, whoever wanted more could get up and take it.

Darkness appeared through the windows and the children got ready for bed. Next to his bed, Natek found a bundle of plans wrapped in brown paper with a note stuck to it in Korczak's handwriting: *"For you to look at. I'd be glad to hear if you have any suggestions for improving the interior design of the rooms."*

Natek opened the plans and saw they were the plans of the orphanage in Warsaw. His eyes caressed the delicate sketches and his finger passed over the outlines of the rooms. He closed the plans, put them reverently under his pillow and fell asleep.

THE RABBIT
AND THE OLYMPICS

All the children were waiting for the summer. It was 1932 and the Olympics were about to take place in Los Angeles. Several months previously, Korczak had already gathered all of them together and announced: "If adults have Olympics – so should children."

After months of anticipation, summer finally arrived, bringing a week of sports contests. "Children are adults with short legs," Korczak told them. And they are now proving it: They are about to be the first children in the world to participate in a children's Olympics!

The home was prepared for the Olympics ahead of time. A month before, Korczak had asked the children to choose a "Committee for Suitable Games," which would determine the categories in which they'd compete. There were running contests, long jump, high jump, group ball games, and even a spoon race, in which the children had to reach the finish line holding a spoon in their mouths with an egg in it. An equally strange contest was the sack race in which children had to hop to the finish line in a sack. There were separate contests for boys and girls as well as mixed contests.

Similarly to the adult contests, there were three stages to the contests: Quarter finals, semifinals, and finals. The committee determined everything. Korczak was thrilled to see them running it all independently and, as usual, he gave them a free hand.

On the morning of the contests, the children awoke with anticipation. There was a lot of tension in the air: Quarrels, shouts, and cries of excitement. In the girls' dormitory, Tzila awoke to the sound of shouting coming from both the girls' and the boys' dormitories. Tzila had come to the orphanage two months before. She'd been placed in Korczak's care by her grandmother.

When she first entered the orphanage, what she noticed at once was the fellowship among the children, which found expression in the quiet that prevailed in the home. A quiet she wasn't used to.

Shouts always distressed Tzila. In her grandparents' home, where she'd grown up before coming to the orphanage, there was constant shouting. She slept in a tiny room with the other cousins whom their grandparents were raising in reduced circumstances. Tzila's parents had died, and she'd spent many days wandering the streets without any proper care. The quiet in the orphanage calmed her but today, she got up to commotion yet again. What was going on?

Dvorah, her mentor in the home, who helped her adjust to the rules and discipline, immediately joined her, hugged her, and said: "Listen to their voices, Tzila. They're shouting but they're happy. The big day we've been waiting for has come – our children's Olympics is beginning!" Then she continued talking about her favorite subject: "Let's show the boys we're just as good as they are." Dvorah was always in competition with the boys, and it was very important to her to show them that the girls were their equals in wisdom, beauty, and now in sport.

Tzila reluctantly got up. It was hard for her to imagine a branch in which she could win. And beat a boy?!

A whistle blew to signal the start of the Olympics. The children were divided into the groups they'd chosen and Tzila felt disconnected. She hadn't registered for any contest because she knew she'd lose. All her life she'd suffered from hunger and, relatively short and thin for her age, she'd never been sports-minded. Once, a long time ago, when she'd still gone to school, the gymnastics classes were only a source of frustration for her. Once school was closed to her, and she'd been forced to wander the streets for most of the day, there'd been occasions when she'd had to run, fast too, but that was to escape from people who wanted to harm and harass her. She remembered how while running, she'd sometimes imagine the story her parents used to tell her – "Alice in Wonderland" – in which the white rabbit always ran and ran and was always late. Always in a hurry to get somewhere else.

So Tzila's thoughts wandered as the contests went into high gear. Tzila sat on the side, gazing at the long jump contest and thinking to herself: "I'll never manage to beat all these enormous children. One step of theirs is like three of mine."

"Hey Tzila, come to the contest. You're signed up for the sack race!" Someone suddenly called out to her. It was yellow-haired Zvi, and just the sound of his sweet voice saying her name almost made her choke with excitement. "Come on, Tzila, you'll be good at this contest. You have to come!" Zvi laughed and went on: "Maybe you'll manage to save the girls. At the moment we boys are in the lead in almost all the contests."

The other children began to shout encouragement: "Tzila! Tzila! Tzila!" Dvorah, her mentor, red and perspiring, popped up suddenly out of nowhere and explained to her what was happening: "Each of the children was registered for some event. It's important to us to win as a group too, not only as individuals. Especially as it's against the boys!" As usual, Dvorah emphasized the issue closest to her heart. "You're registered for this event, Tzila. You probably registered and forgot. Come on," she pulled Tzila's hand.

"I'm registered? Who registered me? I didn't register for anything," replied Tzila, going up to the list, where she saw her name among all the contestants in the sack race. "I wonder who registered me for the contest! There must be some mistake!"

"Come on, everyone's waiting for you!" Cried the children.

"Alright, I'll participate," mumbled Tzila. "I can get into a sack better than anyone because I'm the smallest here."

The contest began, together with shouts and cries of

encouragement. The boys encouraged the boys' group, and the girls encouraged the girls' group. Tzila hopped lightly and fast. Just hearing her name shouted by the cheering girls: "Tzila, Tzila," filled her with strength and, like the beloved rabbit from the book "Alice in Wonderland," she hopped again and again. She imagined herself in a jacket, holding a watch on a chain, and she was late and had to run, hop actually, and fast.

When she went up to receive first prize from the doctor, in the name of the girls' group, she felt a little tap on her back. The doctor ruffled her hair and said: "Well? Is it all right that I registered you?"

Tzila laughed and asked shyly: "Doctor, can I ask you for something? As a girl who took the girls' team to victory?"

"You've earned it, champion. You can ask me for anything," responded the doctor.

"When we've finished reading 'Oliver Twist' in storytime, can you start reading us 'Alice in Wonderland'?" Korczak saw her beseeching eyes and felt instinctively that she'd been read this book by people who were dear to her.

"Of course, Tzila. Gladly," Korczak nodded, hugging her, trying not to show her that he'd noticed the tears that suddenly filled her eyes. And he added: "Now I must run, run quickly, to see if tonight's special meal for all the champions is ready." Jokingly, he pretended to run and disappear from Tzila's eyes.

THE BOYS' SECRET

It was late afternoon on a particularly hot day in August and the mosquitoes were buzzing in the ears of the children as they played in the huts at summer camp. A rumor spread among the boys that they'd be going out on a field trip that night. The boys were thrilled to know that only they would be going out with Korczak and so they kept the secret with hidden joy while exchanging frequent glances and winks.

"Pssst! Leon. Come here," Korczak whispered to Leon, who sat reading a book. Leon was the youngest in the group. A thin slight boy, he approached Korczak, and they whispered together, seeming to come to an agreement about something. They had difficulty keeping the secret and not talk too much, pretending they were each busy with their own affairs.

That night, the boys got into bed fully dressed in warm clothing. Towards midnight, they crept out of bed and quietly slipped away, careful not to wake the girls. One of the new counselors joined them and went downstairs with the boys, where they stood in a group, staring in amazement at the sight that met their eyes: Leon was coming out of the kitchen through a small window. And who was waiting for him outside the window? To the amazement of the children, it was none other than the doctor himself. He was standing at the window, helping Leon smuggle food out of the kitchen.

The two "burglars" took several loaves of bread, butter, jam, and a lot of potatoes for roasting on a fire later that night. Korczak walked about as if he were first among the rogues. His eyes were sparkling with excitement, and he had a broad smile on his face.

There was magic in the darkness of the night, they all felt. The boys, 51 in number, began to walk toward the forest in a group. It was very dark outside, stars peeping out between the light clouds in the sky, and, like a solitary street lamp, the moon illuminated everything. A whole night spent with Korczak, without the girls. A dream come true!

The sound of trampled leaves was strange, the sounds of night animals echoed from far away, and the chorus of crickets seemed to be there, like sweet music, just for the line of children. Only when they reached the heart of the forest did they burst out in a shout of laughter. They'd tried so hard to keep the secret, and now they allowed themselves to relax. Great joy filled them all.

Each one carried equipment on their back: wood for a fire, food, or blankets. Korczak led the group confidently into a forest clearing. And if there was something scary about walking through the dark forest, their elation erased all fear.

Mossek pointed to a purplish light shining out from among the trees and asked Korczak what it was. "I will explain when we're all seated," said Korczak. It's a special phenomenon of the trees." Suddenly, the children noticed a myriad of strange lights circling above them. They were alarmed, but Korczak explained to them that it was glowworms that produce light by means of electric signals from their bodies, and there was no reason to be afraid.

In the clearing, the group sat in a circle, and, instructed by Korczak, they all lay on the ground and listened to the night sounds. The children were used to the sounds and sights of the forest by day while walking nearby, but in the quiet of the night, in the thick of the forest, other sounds were heard. Suddenly the trees looked like the masts of haunted ships, and the rustling in the treetops sounded like the waves of the sea. The dark shades of the leaves were strange. Everything was different and mysterious.

Korczak turned to one of the children and said: "Mossek, you asked about that purplish color coming from among the trees. Well, some trees have a substance called phosphorous. When the phosphorous inside the tree breaks down, it shines, and then we see a kind of light flashing from the tree." They all listened intently to his explanation. Korczak found interest everywhere and in every phenomenon, and he also knew how to talk about these things in an interesting way. As usual, the children were fascinated by his explanation.

In conclusion, he added: "Everything you hear and see

here has a scientific explanation, so there is no reason to be afraid. It's good to know the forest at night too."

The boys began to disperse, each to their own tasks as if they knew exactly what to do. Some children built a small fire and began to roast potatoes on the fire, the wonderful "kartofla." The other, younger children sang amusing songs, their loud voices seeming to indicate they had lost all fear of the dark forest. In the meantime, the older children handed out the food that Korczak and Leon had "filched" from the kitchen.

All their imaginations were busy, especially among the younger children, who had moved away from the fire. They'd heard the sounds of dogs, or could it be lions? Korczak had a special trumpet with three tones, and the children were familiar with its sound from a distance, so when they heard the trumpet they relaxed and began to go back in the direction from which it came. The food tasted almost like paradise, even tastier than usual.

At the end of the meal, the children sat down in a tight circle around the fire. Their eyes shifted between the fire and the doctor's face as he told them stories. Korczak loved telling the children stories about the past, about the days of the wars in which he'd participated. He would spice up the stories with jokes and funny songs he made up.

The hours flashed past, the younger children fell asleep next to the fire, and the others listened to Korczak's stories. Some children were on duty, guarding the group, and every two hours the guards changed.

Just before dawn, the children got in line and began to walk back to the camp. The sounds they'd heard in the night were silent and, instead, came the sound of morning birds, chirping in the ears of the young invaders. Some were cautious and some were carefree. There were lizards everywhere, mice went into their holes, and a light wind blew softly. Swarms of ants came out of their nests for another day's work.

"Children, look at the ants," said Korczak. "See how early in the morning they start preparing food for themselves for the winter." Korczak enjoyed researching ant life, telling the children again and again to learn the value and benefit of hard work from the ants.

The children listened quietly to the sounds of morning, while Korczak found more and more phenomena around them to explain reciprocity in nature. "You'll understand," said Korczak, "I'll give you an example: Geckoes eat butterflies but also flies and other insects. They themselves are eaten by birds of prey, hedgehogs and also other animals. Hedgehogs eat little animals, including geckoes and insects. That's the circle of life in nature." Korczak went on talking until they reached the camp.

The children remembered the sentence he'd said when they'd set out on their night walk: "There is no reason to fear the forest, but you need to know it." And indeed, after the thrilling night they'd experienced, they felt safe.

The group approached the camp. Shmulik placed the doctor's trumpet with its three tones in his mouth and blew forcefully, telling the children who'd stayed home, particularly the girls: "We're on our way home."

Weary but satisfied by the experience, the mischievous boys trailed filthy but happy after Korczak. A surprise was waiting for them when they reached the farm: The counselors and the girls stood there with alarmed faces: Someone had broken into the farm and stolen food from the kitchen. They'd been robbed!

The faces of the boys flushed slightly, Korczak smiled and said soothingly: "Dear friends, nobody broke into the kitchen. We took supplies with us to the forest for a night meal. Since the kitchen was already closed, I sent a child into the kitchen through a window, and I told him what food to take."

"I'm putting myself on trial. I'm the guilty one, just me!" The girls opened their eyes with astonishment and envy.

The next day at breakfast, the boys were talking about the wonders of the night events, and the girls sat there with sour faces. Rocha'leh, a natural leader, sat among them, her mouth tight with envy. In passing, Korczak whispered something in her ear. She smiled from ear to ear and began to pass the message. That very night the girls were going on a field trip with Korczak. Only the girls. The boys continued their chatter and didn't notice the fresh secrets and winks being exchanged behind them.

The children cherished the experience of their night field trip in the forest clearing.

THE MAGICAL VEGETABLES

Korczak wrote a book called "Kaitush the Wizard," saving it especially for camp because the book was a long one, and he wanted to have enough time to read it to the children every Sabbath and to hear their opinions.

The children sat excitedly in the hall. Korczak, facing them, was also excited. He was about to read them the first chapter. Korczak knew he was fortunate; as a writer, he could read his new stories to the children at the orphanage he ran. The children's responses shed another light on things he already knew, maybe too well, in the writing process. The children deepened his understanding of the story he himself had written. He often changed stories before they were printed according to the children's comments or because of things they didn't understand.

The book tells the story of Kaitush the Wizard, who

has a double, about his love for Zosia, and about all sorts of amusing and weird adventures he has. This time, while reading, Korczak and the children invented new scenes. The children were absorbed in the story, particularly mischievous Shlomo, whose nickname was Shlemik, and who loved wizards and adventures and who was loud in his comments: "That couldn't possibly happen! That's an exaggeration. Change the story to..." And, as usual, Korczak listened attentively to his young editors.

When they finished reading, as always – dinner, and each child to his bed. Each child to his dreams. If every child in the world has dreams, the children at the orphanage had twice as many! They dreamed about an ordinary family with two parents and, perhaps, a brother or sister. Or even many brothers and sisters. Some dreamed about visits to distant lands they'd read about in the many books in their library. Above the children's beds floated dreams about heroes and wizards, princes and princesses. Each of them according to the scope of their imagination.

And there were some who dreamed about food. Shlemik was among the first to dream about food. Every night he dreamed about another dish, each one more tempting than the last. That day, immediately after he lay down in bed, he began to dream. In his dream, he became Kaitush, the omnipotent wizard, Kaitush who performed extraordinary magic. In his dream, the most unique foods appeared to him from all over the world, and if he didn't want them, he waved his wand and turned them into something tastier. He turned the noodle pie into an enormous, layered, chocolate cake piled high with strawberries and mountains of cream.

The meatballs prepared by the cook instantly became chocolate ice cream with tiny candies, and the croutons became soft, chewy candies.

And then, in his dream, he saw a huge, red, shiny tomato and a green juicy cucumber. When he bit into the shining vegetables with their special colors, Shlemik felt he could taste paradise. He felt that whoever tasted the special tomato or the cucumber would be healed of any illness and become strong and tall. Shlemik woke and continued to mull over the strange dream. He rubbed his smooth skin and touched his forehead. "Hey, where's the bump I had yesterday?" He remembered how he'd fallen from the huge tree and an enormous bump had swelled up on his forehead where he'd hit his head. Wonder of wonders! His forehead was smooth! No swelling at all!

Shlemik was amazed. What a strange dream! Had he really eaten healing vegetables? He went downstairs, feeling his way in the dark. Everything was dark. Only the doctor sat in a corner, writing in his small handwriting in his journal, probably another one of his stories.

"What happened, why did you wake up? What's bothering you?" He asked Shlemik, whose face seemed confused. Shlemik jumped onto the doctor's lap and stroked his pointed beard. The point of the beard soothed him, like a tiny shot of encouragement. Shlemik calmed down in Korczak's arms. The doctor's embrace was a healing one. Exactly the same feeling as eating the magic vegetables.

"I had a really weird dream. I dreamed I was a wizard, just like Kaitush, the wizard in your story, and I wanted to be as tall as a wizard because I'm really a little short. So the wizard, me, decided this time to eat healthy, magic vegetables." Shlemik continued in his high voice: "Anyone who ate the vegetables would live forever. Very tasty vegetables that can heal any illness, make short children taller, and that are even tastier than a chocolate cake, cream, strawberries, and tiny candies."

Korczak smiled, looking at Shlemik with mischievous eyes. "Shlemik, my little wizard, let's go outside for a few moments. I want to show you something."

Outside it was dark and silent. Only crickets chirped loudly, wondering at the nocturnal visit of the two. Stars shone brightly as if hinting at a secret, and the full moon smiled, joyfully illuminating their steps along the path.

Korczak went to the garden and in the middle, he bent over and picked a long green cucumber and a large, fresh, red, and shining tomato. He skipped to the kitchen and in a few seconds prepared a small salad for Shlemik. He finished it off with a few drops of olive oil. Korczak added olive oil to every meal, telling the children: "Olive oil is good for your health. Drink plenty of olive oil and you'll be as strong as the Greek God, Apollo."

"Come, my little friend, sit down," said Korczak. Putting his warm hand on Shlemik's shoulder, he gently sat him down on one of the dining room chairs. Little Shlemik began to eat the salad. "It really does taste like paradise," he murmured.

"You know," said Korczak, "everything we grow in the vegetable garden with love, we get back with all the healing qualities and taste of paradise. That's the magic."

Shlemik finished eating, feeling he'd had the most sumptuous meal in his life. He patted his little belly and ran off to bed.

Early the next morning, Miss Stefa went downstairs and saw a mess. Who left the kitchen like that? Why was the cutting board dirty? And who hadn't cleaned the oil stains from the table?

Stefa looked angrily at Korczak, but he winked at her. She smiled, winked back, and hummed to herself: "Someone had a night adventure. Interesting..."

The two exchanged a look, they had no need of words. The rules at the orphanage and, of course, at camp, were usually strict. If Korczak broke them, it meant that one of the children had needed something special.

The children woke up, ate, got ready and began to do house chores. Some of them cut fruit and vegetables that had ripened in the garden and put them into small cartons. They loaded the cartons onto the cart that took them to the train and from there to the orphanage in Warsaw, where the cook was glad to store the goods in the storeroom. She liked making the children food from these vegetables because they really did have a special taste – the taste of health.

Some of these magical vegetables were sent to the market in Warsaw. You'll probably guess who sat next to the driver who took the products to market! Yes, you guessed right. Shlemik! He sat on a little cushion, holding the whip in his hand like a wand. Strong, healthy, and proud, he drove the horse to the city, crying "giddyup!"

Once the vegetables were sold and the money collected

that would help fund the orphanage, Shlemik got into the cart and within a few minutes fell asleep and dreamed all the way back. What did he dream about this time?

THE THREE MUSKETEERS

One morning, reinforcements arrived at the summer camp – the three musketeers – three new, eighteen-year-old counselors: Adam, Hannah, and Bernard. Stefa received them at the orphanage in Warsaw and accompanied them to the summer camp.

Adam was short and when the children crowded around him, he was swallowed up amongst them. Bernard was tall, and noble, with broad general knowledge and a tough expression. Hannah was a plump girl who always had a smile on her face. She had fair hair and the children called her "angel" because of the love she lavished on them and her welcoming face.

The three were Korczak's students at the Faculty of Social Sciences at one of the colleges in Warsaw. Their work as an auxiliary force at the orphanage and summer camp at Rozyczka was part of their teacher training. This training program was known as the "Bursa." Counselors were generally called "Bursists," but the children didn't call them by that name. The moment they arrived at the summer camp, the nickname that stuck to them was: "The Three Musketeers."

During the first days, the Bursists worked almost without guidance. They helped with the various groups, in the dining room, organizing outings, and in the yard, as well as hikes in nature. They felt they were "drowning" in their tasks but there was no one to guide them. After a week, Korczak and the other counselors began to help them. They taught them what was necessary and appropriate, discussed with them any difficulties they encountered, and gave them feedback that was sometimes positive and sometimes less so.

Gradually, once they started getting beneficial guidance, the Bursists felt that the initial stage of "drowning" had been an excellent stage in their process of fitting into the home.

They learned to know the ways of the farm and what went on both in and outside of it. They learned to know the children and their personalities. They knew which of them was talented at sport, who loved listening to stories, who needed more warmth and love and who less (and who shrank from such expressions), and who needed a clear framework of discipline and boundaries. They felt that Janusz Korczak, who "abandoned" them at first to experience things for themselves, had chosen the best way to train them in counseling.

They realized that if they respected the way in which he

educated children and, probably, themselves too, he would lead them to success.

When they were alone and couldn't be overheard, the good-hearted Hannah said proudly to her two friends: "We're in good hands!"

Every day they worked with the children accompanied by close supervision that included personal sessions with the counseling team and a weekly session with Stefa (who had also come to the camp that year), and Korczak.

Gradually, the young educators became familiar with Korczak as a therapist and educator. The three observed the children throughout all the hours of the day, and so got to know them in varying situations.

Adam, who had grown up in a simple, poor Jewish home, understood the psyche of the children better than all of them. Particularly children who had difficulty trusting, who didn't always tell the truth, and who occasionally provoked each other. The children slowly grew closer to the slight counselor who accepted them just as they were.

Bernard opened up an enormous, broad, and diverse world of knowledge for the children. He went out into the fields with them, where he told them about nature, the earth, clouds, and earthquakes. He told them about the histories of the various nations in the world and talked to them about any subject they wished. The children sat in perfect silence, and if one of them disturbed the class or made a noise, Bernard immediately and fearlessly scolded them. Bernard attributed great importance to rules. That was how he himself had been raised and it was his way –

to give all his knowledge, as well as demand respect and attention.

Hannah liked all the children, from the smallest to the eldest. She took an interest in each of them and would hug and kiss them all. Warmth and love were necessary and desired in the home, and she gave it to them unconditionally. When she took them to the River *Wisła, the entire group* would sit quietly on the riverbank where they'd observe the sun's rays on the water and enjoy the landscape and the quiet, the perfectly coordinated warmth and love that flowed straight into their hearts from the river and the camp.

Korczak observed the three young counselors and their relationships with the children in the home. He remembered how when he started out, he loved unconditionally like Hannah; later on his educational path, he became as attentive and understanding as Adam; and now, as someone who had accumulated experience, he was as knowledgeable as Bernard. Korczak sighed to himself: "How many years it had taken to acquire the knowledge inherent in each of the three counselors."

Even after many years in education, Korczak still noted down the problems raised by the counselors at the weekly meetings with him and felt he was learning from his students and their diverse approaches. Thanks to them, he too was becoming a better educator. Korczak asked himself, what was better? Was any one educational method better than another? If one day he'd have to choose one of the counselors, which one would he choose? And why? Would he in fact be able to choose? Each of them was an inseparable part of him and, today, he was the whole that included the ways of all three.

Adam, who was the most organized of the three, would make orderly lists of things. During one of his personal conversations with Korczak, he was so impressed by a sentence the doctor said to him, that he noted it down in his journal and read it to his friends: *"Thanks to theory, I know, thanks to practice, I feel. Theory enriches the intellect (knowledge), practice gives color to feeling and forges the will."*

During their leisure hours, the three discussed these sentences. They each had thoughts and ideas of their own and, of course, they didn't always agree.

One day, the younger children went out with Korczak and the three counselors on a day's outing on the river. It was a particularly hot day and Korczak considered canceling the trip, but since he'd already ordered a boat for the day, and not wanting to disappoint the children, he decided to go ahead with the trip.

Early in the morning, the children left home, each with a heavy knapsack full of equipment: Mats, cooking utensils, games, and food and water for the whole day. The children walked heavily towards the river and the boat that would take them sailing. There was a lot of excitement in the air, and they sang songs and told jokes.

After walking for about half an hour, the children were tired, the sounds of laughter and singing faded and they continued walking in silence toward the river. From time to time, they stopped to drink cold water. Bernard's voice was occasionally heard encouraging a child.

When they finally reached their destination, they saw

the boat before them, standing by a steep bank. On the bank was a plank that stretched to the boat deck. The children would have to cross this shaky plank, crossing cautiously, one after another, in order to board the boat.

The children lined up, each carrying a heavy knapsack on their backs, their cheeks flushed, their legs tired and trembling, but their eyes shining and their hearts full of anticipation and the will to conquer the river.

Korczak who was tired, stood at the end of the line, worriedly observing the children. His sharp eyes also examined the behavior of the three counselors. He missed nothing. Despite his great experience as an educator, Korczak was very concerned and felt equally responsible for the children and the team.

Adam, who was barely visible among the children and whose voice was swallowed up among theirs, stood at the head of the line, holding out a hand to each child, helping them board the boat.

Bernard, his head above them all, was clearly heard, certain and encouraging: "Genya, come on, I'll help you. Ruti, come to me, jump and I'll pass you along. Shlemik, wait, don't push! Tamar, drop Brenda's hand, you're only hampering her. Come children, we're almost there!"

Hanna stood at the end of the line. Flushed, her eyes worried, she gazed at the line of children climbing slowly toward the boat. She was holding several knapsacks that she'd taken from the weaker children, and she radiated warmth and love for them. She didn't talk, there was no need. The children felt her caring, enveloping, and protecting them.

An hour later, when the last child had boarded the boat, Hannah heard Korczak's voice, a soft whisper in her ear: "Well, better now, huh?"

She looked to the side but saw nobody. "Weird," she thought to herself. "Maybe I was just imagining it!"

Korczak was aware of the diverse educational methods of the three counselors. He was glad to see that the three Bursists ran the event with responsibility, indicated by the quiet and speed with which the children carried out their requests.

It was hot outside, the event caused tension and was a little scary, but the three young counselors, whom the children completely trusted, conducted it wholeheartedly. The system for loving children was based on values of respect for children, true authority, and belief in the children's abilities.

Korczak witnessed the educational path of each of the three young counselors: The responsibility that radiated from Adam, the authority from Bernard, and the warmth and love of children that emanated from Hannah.

Once all the children had safely boarded the boat, Hannah finally boarded as well. Korczak breathed with relief. He really wanted to whisper some calming words in her ear but decided not to.

Korczak was last on board.

ONCE WE WERE CHILDREN

It was a Sabbath afternoon. The fields shone and bright green bales of hay were scattered about, in the fields. On the top of a hill was a small house with a red roof and a girl was running, flying a colorful kite.

Cars were driving up the path and doors were excitedly opening, women and men with white hair got out of the car.

Greetings were heard, shouts of joy, kisses, and pats on shoulders.

"How you've changed."

"What's happened to you"?

"Is that you?"

"I can't believe it, I have to sit down. You've grown so lovely."

The group sat down, boys and girls, some required help,

and others gave it. Their love and respect for each other were apparent. They'd come quite a distance, without their partners, for they knew other people wouldn't understand what had happened many years before, nor the unique man who had raised them.

Korczak had raised them to be honest, just and to love mankind. They'd all had a happy and meaningful childhood.

They'd survived with faith in Man, life, truth, and justice. They sat for long hours and reminisced, telling their stories.

 *Unfortunately, I could only imagine this meeting and my listening to their whispered stories.*

Those boys and girls, who were supposed to meet, celebrate and remember the days of their childhood at Janusz Korczak's orphanage, went to their death on August 5th, 1942. They were put on a train that took them to Treblinka.

Dr. Janusz Korczak led them, followed by the children in order of age and, behind them, Miss Stefa and the team of educators. They were accompanied on both sides by Germans with guns.

Korczak could be heard encouraging them, saying: "We'll get there soon..."

These stories are dedicated to their memory.

ACKNOWLEDGEMENTS

I wish to thank the cherished people who contributed to my learning and research. With our help, Janusz Korczak's heritage will be preserved.

First of all, Itzchak Belfer, who accompanied my writing process with good advice, first-hand advice from that eternal child, Korczak.
Unfortunately, Yitzchak did not live to see the printed book, he died peacefully at the age of 98.

Dr. Mali Nevo, she and I together conceived the idea of writing this book.

My partner, Chaim Belfer, who encouraged me to keep writing even when it was difficult.

Dalia Tauber, Chair of the Janusz Korczak Educational Institute in Israel, who contributed a great deal of knowledge.

Yossy and Reuven Nadal, who gave sound advice and told me stories they'd heard from their father, Shlomo Nadal.

And of course, my family, who lovingly accepts the Korczak "bug" that I will probably carry with me forever.

Made in the USA
Middletown, DE
27 August 2023